Jake felt himself
realized what was
floor of the boat ar
tied behind his back. Mr Lopez, meanwhile, was
prodded out of the boat and made to stand on the
log. Their eyes met as he looked down at Jake. He
had an agonized expression on his face and seemed
to Jake to be trying to tell him something, but he
was too concerned with the pain of the rope tightening on his wrists to think what it might be.

Within seconds one of the men had started up
the working outboard motor, another had tied their
canoe on behind and they were off down the little
river. He felt himself being kicked none too gently
by a large boot.

'*Qué tal, Jaime?*' said the man with the gun, which
he was holding in one hand pointing straight at
Jake.

'*Adios!*' said the man, and a smelly canvas sack was
pulled over the top of him.

Jake closed his eyes and waited for the shot, but
nothing happened.

JAKE'S ESCAPE

by

ROBIN HANBURY-TENISON

RED FOX

A Red Fox Book

Published by Random House Children's Books
20 Vauxhall Bridge Road, London SW1V 2SA

A division of Random House UK Ltd
London Melbourne Sydney Auckland
Johannesburg and agencies throughout the world

1 3 5 7 9 10 8 6 4 2

First published in Great Britain by Red Fox 1996

Phototypeset in Baskerville 11 on 12.5 by Intype London Ltd
Printed and bound in the United Kingdom by
BPC Paperbacks Ltd, a member of The British Printing Company Ltd

RANDOM HOUSE UK Limited Reg. No. 954009

Papers used by Random House UK Ltd are natural, recyclable
products made from wood grown in sustainable forests. The
manufacturing processes conform to the environmental regulations
of the country of origin.

ISBN 0 09 955551 4

1
Jake's Father Arrives

One week of the summer holidays had passed and Jake was lying in an old string hammock tied between two apple trees in the orchard. Keith, the farmer's son from next door, had said he would drop in and he was looking forward to the competition they had planned. They had been practising every day with the full-sized bow he had been given for his twelfth birthday and, although neither of them could pull the string back all the way yet, they could both hit the bullseye on the big stuffed target more often than not.

It was good fun having Keith as a neighbour. There was always something interesting going on somewhere on the farm and the boys were allowed to help provided they didn't get in the way. There was also a pond down by the old wood where they went to catch tiddlers and had a camp which they were pretty sure no one knew about. They hoped to be allowed to sleep out there later on if they picked the right moment to ask.

'Hi, Jake! Wake up! I haven't got very long. Dad wants me back by milking time.' Keith was beginning to have to work when they were short handed on the farm. The day before, both boys had been called over to help with a cow that was having trouble calving. It was the first birth Jake had watched and he had felt a bit sick but Keith was well used to all that sort of thing.

'OK, let's get going.' Jake rolled out of the hammock and picked the bow up from the ground below. 'Why don't we have ten arrows each first for practice and then ten each for real. Bet I beat you!'

Although they were the same age, Keith was the bigger and stronger of the two. He had always lived in the country while Jake had spent most of his life in a city. He and his mother, who was an artist, had only moved to the scruffy old farmhouse a year or so before. Since then he had learned a huge amount from Keith. Speaking slowly, but surprisingly clever with his big hands, he would explain how to tie different sorts of knots, open sacks of cattle feed, undo a bale of straw and, after his father had been out rabbiting, how to skin and clean them. That was a job Jake had not enjoyed, but the boys' ambition was to practise until they were good enough to go hunting with the bow and arrows, get a rabbit and cook it at their camp.

'You going to be here all the holidays?' asked Keith.

'Don't know,' replied Jake. 'I expect my Dad will turn up some time. You never know with him. Last year he took me fishing and I caught a two pound trout. Another time we went sailing off the coast of Scotland and I was allowed to steer. There was a storm and that was exciting. We camped on an uninhabited island and ate crabs.'

'You're lucky. My parents never take me anywhere.'

6

'I don't think I'd want to go anywhere if I was a farmer,' said Jake.

Just as Jake had loosed his final arrow into the bullseye to win the match by a close eight hits to seven, Keith's father's voice boomed out from across the hedge and there was no time for a return match. Instead, Jake practised until his arms ached and then climbed back into the hammock and thought about his father. Unlike his mother, who had married a quiet carpenter called Philip, his father had not remarried and Jake was never quite sure what he did. He said he worked for the government and a lot of the time he had to travel abroad, 'as a courier' he had once heard his mother say. That sounded mysterious and exciting. He had decided that his father was a spy but of course couldn't say so.

There were chickens and ducks in the garden and a West Highland terrier, Saki, who was ready to play energetic games with an old tennis ball at any hour, day or night. Saki also had a big rubber ball which he couldn't quite get his teeth around so that he had to dribble it like a footballer. Swinging in his hammock, Jake kicked it off into the bushes and knew it would take Saki some time to manoeuvre it back to him. Jake loved it in the country and was never bored, but his mother and stepfather were always so busy with their work that he sometimes felt in the way.

He wondered what his father was doing and if he was going to see him this holidays. Usually there was no warning. He just appeared, though sometimes he telephoned first. His mother and Philip never seemed to mind him being suddenly taken away and for a time he had resented this, wanting his parents to fight over him. Now he didn't care so much and as he dozed in the sun he began to pretend he could hear the sound of a car engine; or perhaps it was a helicopter. It would be just like his father to arrive by helicopter.

He awoke with a start as something heavy landed on his lap. For a moment he thought it was one of the chickens jumping up; he had heard something scratching about nearby as he dropped off to sleep. But it was too small and hard to be a chicken and as his hand closed over it he knew at once what it was — the thing he really wanted — a Swiss Army knife. Not any old Swiss Army knife but the top of the range with thirty-one features. He had told his father who had said that they were far too expensive. He looked up grinning and said 'Thanks, Dad.'

He was so busy opening and closing the different blades, screwdrivers, saws and files he hardly heard what his father said next and asked him to repeat it.

'Wanna go on a trip?'

'You bet! Where to?' Jake replied enthusiastically, putting the knife away in his pocket.

'South America. I'm taking a proper holiday for once and, as I'm broke and can't afford one, I've agreed to give a series of lectures on part of the QE2 world cruise. They fly me and a companion out and back free. It would be great if you came as my companion.'

Jake's mother knew it wasn't worth arguing when the two of them burst in to her studio to tell her. In fact, she had an important exhibition coming up and was glad of the freedom Jake's absence would give her to work harder, though she would never have admitted it.

'Are you sure it's safe?' she asked, a bit half-heartedly.

'On the QE2! You must be joking,' replied her ex-husband cheerfully, and within the hour Jake had packed a few clothes, his passport and the new knife, kissed his mother, hugged the dogs and they had left.

They took a train to London where they stayed for a couple of days in his father's flat. There were visas to get, some shopping to do — 'Got to make you presentable for the QE2. Everyone gets dressed up really smartly when they're at sea, so they say,' his father told him — and they had a chance to see a couple of new films together. It was all a bit of a rush and Jake was quite glad when he had to spend an hour or so alone in the flat while his father went out to do some business. It gave him a chance to examine the knife properly and read the booklet he had been given with it. Some of the gadgets took a bit of working out but he enjoyed imagining how he would use them. He cut his finger and toe nails with the scissors, something he was not usually too keen on; peered at minute things on the floor through the powerful magnifying glass; and practised opening a tin with the tin opener. It was exciting to read about how similar knives had saved peoples' lives, including unblocking a climber's oxygen system at the top of Mount Everest.

They flew to Los Angeles and went straight on board. The ship, as their taxi dropped them on the dock, loomed over them. Jake had never seen anything as big in his life.

'Gosh!' he whispered, 'I'll bet that doesn't do many miles to the gallon.'

'Actually, she does just fifty metres to the gallon of diesel and they use a thousand tons of fresh water a day — that should be enough to keep even you clean,' answered his father. 'She's nearly three hundred metres long and there are thirteen decks,' he went on, quoting from the manual they had received with their tickets.

Jake counted the portholes, which got bigger and bigger up the ship's side, ending in huge square ones below the row of enormous lifeboats.

'I hope we sink and have to use those,' said Jake.

'I very much hope not!' said his father.

'We might hit an iceberg, like the Titanic.'

'Unlikely, as we're heading south in the Pacific Ocean and will cross the equator in a few days. You wait, there's so much to do on board that the last thing you're going to want is to be wrecked.'

And so it turned out. Jake just couldn't believe how many things were going on. With four swimming pools and food being served all over the place at all hours — and all free — he thought he would never have time to do all the swimming and eating he wanted to pack in. Life with his mother was great, but there was nowhere to swim except the duckpond, and there you had to wade out through the mud, and meals at home did tend to be a bit scrappy. He had never eaten really good food before and, after the shock of the first dinner, when he had peered suspiciously at what was put in front of him and asked if there was any tomato ketchup, he had begun to experiment and enjoy the different tastes. When he had stuffed himself until he couldn't eat another steak or prawn or peach, or even one of the chocolate coins in gold wrapping which miraculously re-appeared in their cabin every time he emptied the plate, he started exploring and making friends with the crew. They were all really friendly and, as there were few other children on board, they let him get away with murder.

There were secret doors he learned to recognize but which the other passengers never noticed. These led to staircases down to the crews' quarters where his friends covered for him so that sometimes he was able to eat with them. That was much more fun than the grand dining rooms. He managed to sneak into the kitchens and even to peep into the vast and frightening engine room where *absolutely no one was allowed*. There were nine colossal marine engines, the largest ever built. Each was as big as a double-decker bus and weighed over 400 tons. One of the engineers told him that they could push the ship along at more than 32 knots flat out if they really needed to (he worked out that that was 37 miles an hour, which is pretty fast for a ship), but that they normally cruised at a more economical 28.5 knots. There were lots of other huge and fascinating machines down there which he would have loved to investigate, including the one which converted 1000 tons of sea water into fresh water each day, but one of the senior officers spotted him and he was told that if he was caught in there again he would be keelhauled. He was not sure what this meant and later asked his father.

'What have you been up to?' he asked. 'It must have been something pretty bad! It's what they used to do to really wicked sailors years ago. They were

tied by the feet and hands to long ropes and dragged right round under the ship's keel. Not nice,
especially as the bottom of a ship is usually covered
in sharp barnacles.'

Jake decided not to try getting into the engine
rooms again.

2
Jaime Comes Aboard

In Costa Rica, another twelve year old joined the ship. He was called Jaime, which was pronounced like Hi me!, and at first Jake wasn't sure he was going to like him as he spoke hardly any English, and that very badly. He complained about this to his father.

'So how much Spanish do you speak, clever clogs?' his father retorted, and that afternoon he nerved himself to say '*Buenos dias*' to Jaime. He hadn't realized that the big woman next to him was his mother and he was dreadfully embarrassed when she clasped him to her bosom saying '*Que lindo*!'

Then Jaime grabbed his sleeve, pulled him from his mother's embrace, and they dashed off giggling together and were soon inseparable. Jaime proved unbeatable at ping pong, but Jake had the edge at shuffleboard, which required great restraint when aiming to compensate for the pitch of the deck. Together they were able to explore even more effectively, one distracting a crew member while the other slipped through a forbidden door. Gradually their popularity with the crew waned but Jake's Spanish improved and he even ate at Jaime's table a

13

couple of times and managed to say a few sentences.

His father's first lecture was fairly boring, he thought, being about history and politics, but Jake loyally attended it. He had been proud to see the announcement on the front of the daily programme, which was pushed under their cabin door early each morning.

At 11.00 a.m. in the Theatre
CONQUERORS AND DIPLOMATS OF SOUTH AMERICA
*A fascinating illustrated survey of the chequered history of this turbulent
continent seen through the eyes of a traveller*
by
Peter Travis

There had been rather too many pictures of early presidents and Spaniards with little beards, who all looked alike to Jake, and not enough about where his father had actually been. Lots of people asked questions and he was impressed by how much his father seemed to know, but no one asked anything interesting, like whether they wore all that armour in the jungle or how much blood there was when they cut each other's throats, and Jake slipped out to look for Jaime.

He found him, as he had thought he would, up on the Signal Deck helping to feed the dogs. They had made friends with the kennel keeper, an old sailor called Giles, who had been doing the job for twenty years, and he let them exercise the dogs on the enclosed deck where they were allowed to run.

There was a white Chelsea lamp-post there for the male dogs to raise their legs on and plenty of room to run around. They were not a very impressive collection, two small poodles and a very old dachshund, but it was exciting to be somewhere none of the other passengers knew about and a good excuse to throw a tennis ball to each other without getting in anyone's way. The dogs loved it and raced around enjoying the freedom from their small cages.

Giles was full of stories about exciting things that had happened on the QE2 — and things that might happen. 'What about pirates?' the boys wanted to know. 'Have you ever been boarded?'

'Not yet, we haven't,' said Giles, 'and I hope we never are. There are lots of pirates around today, more than at any time since the bad old days of Captain Morgan, especially in the South China Seas and off the coast of Africa. But we'll be ready for them if they try it on.'

'What would you do? Have you many, many guns?' Jaime asked excitedly.

'We have, but we would rather not use them. Much too dangerous. No, our best defence is our Mark One Eyeball.'

'What on earth is that?' asked Jake, imagining a huge satellite dish with fixed death ray.

'That's what we call a lookout,' Giles replied. 'All the time we are in pirate waters we have at least one man on watch at the stern.'

'But what would you do if he saw a pirate ship approaching?'

'Ah, we have several tricks up our sleeves. First, we would make a screen of water with our fire hoses

15

around the ship so that they would be wet and con-fused before they reached us. Then, if they tried to climb aboard, we'd flush them away with a direct jet. No one can face that.'

Jake and Jaime decided that they would pretend to be pirates and see if they could get to the bridge without being seen. From the kennel deck they were able to have a good look around some of the higher parts of the ship where passengers never went and where there was nobody around most of the time. That afternoon they slipped back into the kennels when Giles wasn't looking and scrambled up to the deck above. Creeping along out of sight they were able to look down on the open wings which stretched out on either side of the bridge. There was a great view from up there. They were in front of the huge single red funnel and the wind was strong in their faces.

'Let's give them a big *sorpresa*!' Jaime said, and they jumped down onto one of the wings.

A very surprised first officer of the watch and a young coxswain looked at them in amazement. For a moment no one moved, then just as the officer was reaching for the telephone and the boys were realizing that they were in serious trouble, a door opened and the captain walked in accompanied by the second officer of the watch. The captain was enormous and took in the situation at once.

'Get them!' he said, quietly.

The young officer at his side moved quickly and the boys found themselves suspended by the scruffs of their necks like two puppies, one in each hand.

'And just what do you think you are doing?' the captain asked ominously.

'Sorry sir', said Jake. 'We were pretending to be pirates and to see if we could take the bridge.'

'Well, you nearly did,' the captain replied. 'I can see I'm going to have to tighten up on security around here. How did you do it?'

'It was easy because we've been allowed to help feed the dogs and from that deck there's not a lot of climbing to do.'

'All right. That privilege is herewith removed and I don't want any more trouble from you on this voyage. Is that clearly understood?'

Jake's and Jaime's 'Yes, sir' and 'Si, Señor' came out simultaneously.

'Have you any idea how inconvenient it would have been if one of you had fallen overboard, scrambling about like that?'

'What would you have done if we had?' asked Jake, rather cheekily.

'I'd have had to put the ship into a Williamson Turn,' replied the captain, with a twinkle in his eye. 'That's a very complicated manoeuvre which takes the ship back to exactly where she was, so that we could try and pick you up. But the point is that it would waste a great deal of time and put us behind schedule. Anyway, now you are here you had better have a look round, but for heaven's sake don't touch anything!'

After that the boys had a great time being shown around the bridge. There were all sorts of clever instruments for navigating and telling exactly where the ship was at any moment. They were allowed to sit in the captain's special chair but not to 'drive'.

'I think you have got away with quite enough for one day!' the captain said.

There was a far better view from the bridge than from anywhere else on the ship. Looking right down on the water they were surprised to see how much rubbish there was floating in the sea.

'I'm afraid other ships are not as scrupulous about not discharging their rubbish,' the captain told them. 'On the Queen Elizabeth 2 we take everything home.'

The boys also saw a hump-backed whale which the first officer pointed out to them as it undulated lazily through the water. None of the other passengers had noticed it from the lower decks.

Thanking the captain and other officers as politely as they knew how, they finally left. 'Phew!' said Jake as they raced back to his cabin to tell his father, 'I thought we were in real trouble then. It's lucky we weren't keelhauled.'

'What's that?' asked Jaime, and Jake told him.

One day, after they had been at sea for about a week, the captain made an announcement over the Tannoy.

'Tomorrow morning we will be arriving in Callao, the port of Lima, the capital of Peru. We will moor alongside at seven a.m. and we will be remaining there for twelve hours. Because of the danger from terrorism by the *Sendero Luminoso* or Shining Path guerrillas, I have to advise you that it is dangerous to go ashore. Most passengers will not, I know, be doing so but a few tours been arranged.'

'I didn't know there were gorillas in Peru, Dad,' said Jake.

When he had stopped laughing, his father explained that the captain was referring to rebels who fought a constant battle against the Peruvian government. It was a horrible war, he told him, in which both sides were ruthless and cruel to their enemies and the poor peasants got caught in the middle.

'Are we going ashore, Dad?' asked Jake.

'I'm afraid not,' said his father. 'I can't stand organized tours, and anyway they are very expensive. It's a pity as I would really like to see some of Peru again. I haven't been here for years.'

Jaime's parents were listening, as they were all sitting at the same table. Señor Alonso Lopez, his father, who spoke good English, said 'Why not fly down with us to our place for the day? I have my own plane in which I can take you and there is a late afternoon commercial flight back which will get you to Lima in plenty of time to be on board by eight o'clock. It is not expensive.'

Jake looked pleadingly at his father. Jaime had told him that there was jungle not far from his house where you could see parrots and monkeys. He really wanted to go there. His father hesitated. It was risky as he well knew: flights over the Andes were unreliable and it would not do to miss the QE2's departure. But it was just the sort of adventure he had promised Jake and it was hard to refuse.

'OK,' he said, 'Let's do it — and thanks, Alonso.'

3
Jaime's Farm

They were the first off the ship next morning. Jaime's parents had a car waiting and they sped to the airport. The plane was a six-seater Piper Aztec so there was barely room for all of them as well as the pilot; but as Jake and his father had no luggage, they managed to squeeze in.

The flight over the Andes was breathtaking with huge snow-covered peaks and deep passes through which they flew, the mountains towering above them on both sides. They then dropped down towards the endless rainforest stretching to the horizon, with glistening rivers meandering through it.

'We're over the watershed now,' said Jake's father. 'That means that all the rivers behind us run back into the Pacific Ocean while those down below us now must run into the Amazon in Brazil and so reach the Atlantic eventually.'

They landed on Jaime's own airstrip beside the Ucayali River beyond Pucallpa.

'Don't worry,' said Senor Lopez. 'I will send you into the airport in my jeep in plenty of time.'

As they circled before landing, Jake saw the tops of the forest trees just below the plane, then cleared forest with jagged stumps showing, then suddenly cattle yards and, startlingly white and close, large horned cattle with humps on their backs.

By now it was mid morning and the heat was terrific. It was like opening the door of a blast furnace as they left the cabin, but across a stretch of open ground lay a long, low house with a red tiled roof and wide verandas covered in creepers. Jaime raced Jake up to it and proudly showed him his bedroom, his scramble motorbike and the ping pong table, on which they were playing by the time the adults arrived in the jeep with the luggage.

'Hey, you two!' called Jaime's father. 'It's too hot for that. What do you say to taking the boat out and going fishing?'

Jake saw Jaime's mother look up sharply and heard her say something rapidly in Spanish. They argued for a while but, to his relief, the father won and soon a picnic was being prepared. Jaime, who had admired Jake's Swiss Army knife very much, said it was good he had brought it as the gadget for taking hooks out of fishes' mouths would be very useful.

'*Hay mucha pesca,*' he said. 'Much fish. *Hay mucho sol tambien. Tú necesitas sombrero.*'

Jake understood that he needed a hat against the sun. In Jaime's room there were lots of hats on a shelf. Jake chose an army camouflage one with pockets in the hat band. These Jaime filled with fish hooks of various sizes, coils of fishing line and some raisins as bait.

Their boat was open, made of aluminium and had two big outboard motors on the back.

'*Muy rápido,*' said Jaime, as they scrambled in and stowed baskets of food and fishing rods. The boatman was small and dark with a terrible squint. Jake whispered to his father that he hoped he could see where he was going.

'He's an Indian,' he replied, 'probably from one of the local tribes, and I expect he knows this river like the back of his hand.'

The Indian was called Manolo. 'Do you know why they're called Indians?' his father asked and Jake remembered the answer from school. 'It's because Columbus thought he had reached India.'

'But do you know why they used to be called Red Indians?' his father asked again and this time Jake was stumped. 'It's because they used to cover their bodies with the juice of a red berry which acts as a good insect repellent. Columbus and his men thought they were really that colour — and they got bitten by all the insects!'

Manolo had no red dye on, but his skin was so wrinkled that Jake reckoned any insect would have a hard time getting through it.

Waving goodbye to Señora Lopez, who stood on the bank looking worried, they sped off down the main river, planing fast over the water. Then, just as Jake was really beginning to enjoy the sensation of flying across the surface, the wind and spray cooling him deliciously, the boat veered in towards the bank and shot into the dark tunnel of a tributary.

At first the trees were high overhead, the water below clear and deep. Gradually the banks began to close in and Manolo had to slow right down as the stream twisted and turned. Now Jake could see fish darting away below, and some of them looked quite big. This was going to be exciting.

They moored at a place where there was a small

lagoon and a gigantic tree had fallen into the water making a perfect platform for fishing. Manolo showed Jake how to fix a raisin to the hook and cast it out into the water without flicking it off. Almost immediately both boys had small fish on, which they dangled from the ends of their rods over the boat for Manolo to remove, or so Jake expected. Instead he forced the hook further through the body of each fish with his knife so that the entrails hung out.

'Ugh!' exclaimed Jake. 'Why's he doing that?'

'*Por las pirañas*,' said Jaime. Jake, who had been dangling his bare feet in the water, understood the word and rapidly withdrew them. He watched as Jaime cast the mangled bait far out and then did the same. Almost at once there was a sharp tug on his line and he began to wind in, shouting 'Hey Dad! Look at this!'

His father, who had gone ashore, came running just in time to see a big ugly piranha, its hideous teeth snapping audibly, lifted out and dangled towards the now rather more careful Manolo.

'Watch out!' shouted his father. 'Those teeth can easily take a finger off. You leave it to Manolo.'

The Indian grasped the line well above the fish and lowered it to the floor of the boat, where there was a wooden deck. He waited until it stopped flapping for a moment and then neatly chopped its head off with the long sharp blade called a machete, which he had in a scabbard on his belt.

He then let go of the line and Jake found himself holding a rod with a fish head on the end.

'What am I supposed to do now?' he asked.

'Throw it back, I suppose,' replied his father and

Jaime nodded encouragingly as he did so. In seconds he had another piranha on the end, but he had to wait while Jaime had his one removed by Manolo.

'This is what I really call fishing,' he yelled to his father. 'Better than those crafty old trout in Scotland any time. And there were midges there.'

'You wait till the mosquitoes start,' answered his father, 'and, anyway, trout taste better.'

But, as it turned out, the piranha were delicious. Jaime's father had made a fire up on the bank out of dead twigs and over it he had built a tripod of green wood from which he suspended the headless bodies of the fish over the fire. The skin soon charred and crinkled back from the juicy white flesh underneath, which they all ate carefully in their fingers, holding the fish in leaves gathered by Manolo, and trying to avoid the many small bones. The piranha were tasty, but this didn't stop the boys tucking in to the feast of good things in the baskets: succulent steaks, roast sweet potatoes and plantains — a sort of vegetable banana, which they cooked in the embers — followed by melons and oranges. Jake and his father agreed it was the best picnic they had ever been on.

After lunch Jaime asked in faltering English, 'Mister Travis. Can you find with me wood for the fire?' and they went off together. Manolo and Jaime's father were tinkering with one of the engines and Jake had a tangle to unscramble in his line. He wanted to get back to fishing. He was thinking how well they all got on together and how nice it would be if Jaime and his family could come and visit them in England — they seemed to be rich enough to do so — when he heard the sound of an outboard motor.

A long thin dugout canoe nosed round the bend into the lagoon and stopped opposite them. In it were three young men in tattered army clothes. Jake noticed that Manolo and Jaime's father had gone very still and were doing nothing to the engine on which they had been working so busily a few moments before. The three newcomers looked shifty. They seemed to be trying to see if there was anyone else in the party, but Jaime and Jake's father were out of sight and earshot, there being no more good firewood near the bank.

Suddenly one of the men pulled back some sacking on the floor of the canoe and lifted up an automatic rifle. He pointed it at the boat and called out 'Señor Lopez!'

Jaime's father said nothing.

'Señor Lopez!' the man shouted again, angrily this time.

Before Mr Lopez could speak, Manolo bent down to reach for something in the bottom of the boat and the gun cracked. In slow motion, Manolo stood up and fell backwards into the water. Blood began to pour from the hole in his back as he lay still, face down. Jake watched numbly; then in growing horror as the body began to twitch and vibrate. He realized that the piranha, attracted by the blood, were starting their terrible work.

There was a rapid exchange of incomprehensible Spanish as the men pushed their canoe across the narrow lagoon and the one with the gun prodded it into Mr Lopez's stomach, hard. Once again he said

'Señor Lopez?' this time quietly, through gritted teeth. And Mr Lopez, after a pause, whispered '*Sí*.'

Jake was standing rigid with shock staring at what was left of Manolo and hardly aware of what was going on around him. He had never seen a dead body before and he felt sick as the thought crossed his mind that it was something he had thought he rather wanted to see. Instead, he just felt shattered at the sudden loss of a life. It seemed so awful and pointless. Nothing else seemed to matter and his head reeled.

Then he felt himself grabbed and, before he had realized what was happening, he was lying on the floor of the boat and his hands were being roughly tied behind his back. Mr Lopez, meanwhile, was prodded out of the boat and made to stand on the log. Their eyes met as he looked down at Jake. He had an agonized expression on his face and seemed to Jake to be trying to tell him something, but he was too concerned with the pain of the rope tightening on his wrists to think what it might be.

Within seconds one of the men had started up the working outboard motor, another had tied their canoe on behind and they were off down the little river. As he strained his neck to look back, Jake glimpsed two figures running out of the trees. Then they were round the corner and out of sight. He felt himself being kicked none too gently by a large boot.

'*Qué tal, Jaime?*' said the man with the gun, which he was holding in one hand pointing straight at Jake.

'*Adios!*' said the man, and a smelly canvas sack was pulled over the top of him.

Jake closed his eyes and waited for the shot, but nothing happened.

4
Kidnapped

His first emotion was pure terror. Nothing remotely like this had ever happened to him. He had been frightened before a few times. Once he had climbed out of his bedroom window on a moonlit night and forced himself to walk down towards the big wood. He had lost his nerve when a cow snorted close to him and he had raced back sure there was something following him. But that had been nothing like as frightening as this. He had just seen someone shot dead and there was every chance he would be next. This was not television or testing himself; this was real. For a time he could do nothing but shake uncontrollably, until another kick shocked and hurt him into lying still.

He took a deep shuddering breath and forced himself to stop seeing Manolo's body in his mind's eye and to concentrate on something else. What was going on? He was puzzled when he tried to work it out. Why had they taken him and why had the man with the gun called him 'Jaime'? In order to take his mind off the pain of the rope, which was now cutting into his wrists, he decided to try and be calm and think it through clearly. It had all happened so quickly. One moment he was having the best day of his life, easily catching and then eating fish from a beautiful Amazonian lagoon; the next he was in the middle of a dark, smelly and very frightening nightmare. Why had the man called him 'Jaime'? True, Jake's hair was dark and he could be mistaken for a Peruvian, he supposed, but he didn't look a bit like Jaime. Yet the man had known that name.

With a sinking feeling, it gradually dawned on him that he must have been kidnapped in mistake for Jaime. There could be no other explanation. Presumably a ransom would be demanded from Jaime's father and, once the men realized that he was not Jaime and that his father was not rich, he would become valueless. Clearly they did not value life highly and he realized that they would probably kill him when they found out the truth. They might send him back unharmed but, after seeing the ruthless way they had gunned down poor old Manolo, who was probably only bending down to pick up a fish from the pile at his feet and offer one to them, he thought it unlikely. What could he do? He wanted to beg them to let him go, to explain that they had made a mistake, to promise anything if they would just free him. But he knew it was no good. He would not be able to explain in his poor Spanish and they would not listen anyway. Also, that would give away the fact that he was not Jaime and as long as they believed he was they might not kill him. He desperately needed someone to help him, a friend to advise him, a grown-up to tell him what to do. But there was no one and he felt very frightened and alone. Nobody was about to come to his rescue. He was on his own and would have to keep his head. Then what? Lying still wasn't going to solve anything. What should he do? Slowly he came to the conclusion that if no one was going to rescue him, he would have to try and escape before they learned the truth.

Escape! He had nothing to escape with. No! That wasn't quite true. He had his Swiss Army knife and his watch. That had a luminous face and he could just wriggle his arms round enough to get a glimpse of it down in the sack behind him. It was a comfort to have even that tiny glimmer of light as company. He would need more than that, though, to escape. He was barefoot and although his feet were quite hard for an English boy, as he usually ran around at home without shoes on, he would not get far in this country without protection. He racked his brains to think where he had put his trainers and prayed that they were still in the boat and not left behind on the shore with the picnic things. With them he might stand a chance; without them he was helpless.

The engine stopped and he lay still in the sudden silence, listening intently and tensed against something painful happening, like being trodden on by one of the men as they moved around the small boat, tipping it violently from side to side. He heard muffled swearing and the tinkle of metal on metal. He guessed that they must be working on the second outboard motor. Suddenly it sprang into life, then the other one started, and at once Jake could feel, from the rapid vibration of the boat below him, that they were moving at high speed.

They must have reached the main river and he tried to guess if they had turned left, upstream and back towards Jaime's farm, or right, downstream and away from hope and safety. Jake knew, from spy stories he had read, that he should be counting so as to be able to work out how far he was being taken, but he felt too frightened, confused and, suddenly, terribly, terribly lonely. To his shame, he found himself sobbing uncontrollably and after a while he fell asleep.

He awoke with a start as the boat bumped to a stop and the engines ceased their roar. Now there were many voices, including a female one which seemed to be asking a lot of questions, although he could not understand the rapid Spanish. He felt himself being lifted out of the boat and carried fore and aft before being dumped hard on the ground. Someone began to fiddle with the string tying the sack around him, the knots were undone and it was pulled off.

He looked up into the face of a beautiful dark girl with long black hair tied in a plait and with very bright, sharp eyes, the pupils flecked with gold. For a moment she stared deep into his eyes and he felt himself almost hypnotized; then her glance flickered over the rest of his face and he realized that his nose had been running and that he must look silly, having been crying and unable to wipe the tears away. For an instant her eyes met his again, without expression, then she turned away and gave hurried orders to those standing around. As she stood up, he saw that she was dressed in dark green army clothes and had a revolver at her waist. She seemed to be in charge.

Lifted to his feet, he was marched by two men, one holding each arm, towards a group of thatched huts. One hut had a tall pole with a radio aerial strung from it to a tree. Another had two camou-flaged tents beside it. They were in a small clearing in the forest beside a deep, narrow stream, clearly not the main river, and there were about a dozen men standing in groups staring at him. Almost all were carrying guns, rifles slung over their shoulders with bandoleers of bullets across their chests. Although most were dressed in ragged jeans and many had beards, there was a feeling of an army camp to the place. These were not simple robbers. These were guerrillas. These were the Shining Path people the captain of the QE2 had warned every-one about.

Not looking where he was going, he stepped on a thorny plant, yelped and almost fell over. He hopped on one foot, holding up the other in which several spines were embedded. The men stopped and, after a shouted exchange, his trainers were, to his great relief, chucked up the bank from the boat. With a laugh, his hat was sent spinning across the clearing after them to land upside down beside him. Written in indelible ink inside the brim was the name Jaime Lopez. At a command from the girl the trainers were brought to him, his hands were untied and he was plainly ordered to put them on. This he did, sitting on the ground and carefully picking out the thorns first, then pulling on his socks which he had luckily stuffed inside the toes when he took the trainers off.

Putting on his hat, he stood up, took out his handkerchief, feeling the knife at the bottom of his deep trouser pocket, wiped his face and blew his nose. Shoving the handkerchief back in his pocket he thought to himself 'No one's going to want to

31

investigate past that now.' He looked defiantly around at his captors and, for the first time since he had been kidnapped, he felt brave. His eyes caught those of the girl leader, who was looking at him intently. For a moment he thought she was going to smile at him, then she barked a command and he was pushed roughly into one of the huts. The door was slammed and bolted behind him.

The hut had a bare floor. A cotton hammock was slung diagonally across in between two of the corner posts. Over it was draped a khaki ground sheet tied at the ends with longer pieces of string stretching to the walls so that he had to duck below them as he crossed the room. This, he realized looking up, was to keep the rain from the many holes in the roof off the hammock. There was a rough wooden chair, a tin basin with some dirty water in it, an empty bucket which stank of pee, a couple of newspaper cuttings pinned to the uneven plank walls – and that was all.

Jake paced once round the room and found a crack near the door, through which he had a view of a small part of the camp. He tried to read the cuttings but could understand little as they were in Spanish. He did see a headline referring to *Sendero Luminoso* which seemed to confirm his suspicions. Gingerly, he lowered himself into the hammock. There was a thin blanket in which he wrapped himself and he lay listening to the noises of the camp outside. Now he began to have doubts about escaping. It would be so much easier just to lie there, close his eyes and hope he would wake up to find it was all a dream. He pulled the blanket over his head and pretended he was at home. After a while he began to doze off.

The door crashing open woke him up with a start. A meal of rice and black beans in a tin plate and a spoon to eat it with were thrust at him. The big man who brought it was grinning happily at him and for a dazed moment Jake thought he was going to be told that the whole thing had been a mistake. The man hung, from one of the beams, a large bunch of green bananas growing from a thick stem. Then, with a quick glance over his shoulder as though he was exceeding his authority, he pulled two packets of chewing gum out of his breast pocket and pressed them into Jake's hand. He hurried out, locking the door behind him. The rice and beans were good, but the bananas were a bit unripe and so Jake only ate one. Back in the hammock, he sat upright now taking deep breaths and beginning to work out how to escape.

The roof looked pretty flimsy and he was sure he could break a hole in it big enough to climb through. But that was likely to be noisy and would not be easy without waking up the camp. He examined the door and saw that the lock was simply a bolt on the outside. It was crudely attached to the door frame by Phillips screws, that is, cross-headed ones. Quickly checking his pocket knife, he sighed with relief at finding that it did indeed have the Phillips screwdriver feature. He was just testing the first screw and had felt it loosen when he heard feet approaching and hurried back to the hammock.

It was the girl. She sat down in the chair and began to talk to him, while he sat on the edge of the

33

hammock with his feet on the ground. Her voice was friendly and she seemed to be trying to reassure him and make him relax. After a while she stopped at what was obviously a question. Jake's heart was beating fast. He had decided that he must not let on that he did not speak Spanish, and so could not be Jaime, so as to delay as long as possible the discovery that he was not a valuable hostage; but this was going to be difficult and he was going to have to act, something he had always felt embarrassed by when made to take part in school plays. Now his life might depend on it and he had to do something. The girl was staring at him waiting for an answer and looking puzzled. He must act or she would smell a rat. Making his face crumple up, he burst into fake tears and buried his face in his hands, sobbing noisily. As he began to feel foolish and unconvincing, he climbed back into the hammock, curled up in a ball and made himself shake, as though terrified. In fact, it wasn't very difficult, he found, to pretend to be cracking up under the strain and he found himself almost believing his own act.

The next thing he knew, his hair was being pulled hard upwards, his face came clear of the blanket and he felt a sharp and extremely painful slap on his left cheek. For an instant he was again looking deep into those flecked eyes, this time exchanging a stare of fury. With a huge effort, he resisted the temptation to punch her full on the nose and instead jerked his hair from her hand. Burying his face again, he found that the slap had brought tears to his eyes and by rubbing them he could make more flow. When he forced himself to glance up appealingly at her like a frightened child, he really did feel that he looked a convincing mess again. She looked speculatively at him and he was not entirely sure that his trick had worked; but she turned on her heel and marched out. He heard the bolt pushed across and lay back stroking his cheek tenderly.

5
Escape

Nobody else came to see him and quite quickly it began to get dark. In a sudden hurry, he began to loosen the six screws holding on the bolt. One was very stiff and he thought it was going to beat him, but by forcing the end of the bottle opener in behind the plate he managed to ease it out and at last he felt it turn. Tightening them up again, he lay down once more to rest. It was as well that he did so, for soon after dark the same man who had delivered his food earlier brought another big plate of rice and beans. This time Jake only ate the beans, filling the wide pockets of his bush shirt with all the rice he could cram in and then buttoning them down. When the man came back to collect the plate, Jake was huddled down in the hammock so that he should not see what a strange shape he had become. Pausing to examine the bolt, while Jake held his breath, he turned, said 'Buenas noches, Jaime' and tossed a packet of boiled sweets into the hammock. 'Gracias,' whispered Jake. The man nodded and was gone.

Jake lay still, listening to the noises of the camp and thinking. He thought he could hear the crackle and whine of a radio transmitter among the voices and clatter of tin plates. He was sure it would not be long before they discovered their mistake and so he must get away as soon as possible. But where should he go? He didn't even know if the guerrillas' camp was on the right or left bank of the main river, the Ucayali; or if he was upstream or downstream of Pucallpa, the town they were supposed to have flown back to Lima from. That plane would have left long ago and, come to think of it, the QE2 would already have sailed without them. He could see from his watch that it was now 9.00 p.m. and she had been due to go at 8.00. His father must be frantic and he was sure everyone would be helping to look for him. But would they be trying as hard for an English boy as they would if the son of a rich and important Peruvian had been kidnapped? Jake rather doubted it.

If he did succeed in getting away from the camp, his captors would expect him to go downstream towards the main river and Jaime's home. Of course, the best plan of all would be to take a boat. But they were sure to be guarded and anyway Jake didn't really know how to work an outboard motor, although his father had let him drive one once in Scotland. Even if he could steal a boat, they would soon catch him when they found he was gone if he was only paddling. He had better follow the tributary upstream until he was well away and then try to work his way across country back to the Ucayali.

Gradually the camp settled down for the night. There were fewer voices. He could hear someone washing tin plates in the river, then whistling as they carried them back across the camp and dropped them on the ground with a crash. Then silence.

His watch said it was still not ten o'clock, but he decided he must wait until midnight before escaping. He put his eye to the crack to see if he could see any lights, but everything was dark. Luckily his watch had a button which lit up its face, but that was all the light he now had.

As he peered through the crack he heard footsteps and glimpsed a sudden light. A few moments later someone tested the bolt on his door. It looked as though they had posted a sentry. During the next two hours his door was rattled three more times. That meant that the sentry did his rounds about every half hour and, since he could not think of a way of doing up the screws again from outside once he had undone them inside, he would probably only have half an hour's start at most if he did manage to escape.

Feeling carefully round the small room in the pitch dark, he assembled his possessions. With his knife he cut the four strings holding up the ground sheet and laid it on the floor. Then he tried to untie the hammock rope. He wished he had thought to do this in daylight as it was quite stiff. At last he found that all he had to do was pull the single end and the knot came undone. Before undoing the other end he carefully felt how it was done and memorized the knot. He rolled the hammock up as tight as he could with the blanket inside, put the bag of sweets in the middle out of temptation's way, folded the ground sheet over it and tied the bundle securely with the string. Jaime's hat he put on his head and then he had a last feel round thinking there must be something else. He quietly tore down a couple of the cuttings, folding them up and tucking them into the bundle. As an afterthought, he prised out half a dozen of the drawing pins thinking they might come in useful. Standing up he bumped into the bunch of bananas. He had forgotten about them. He ate a couple to give himself strength and then tried carrying the thick stalk in one hand and the bundle in the other. He reckoned he could run quite fast like that, if only he could see where he was going.

He looked out of the crack again and thought someone had turned a light on. He could see a man walking towards the hut and it dawned on him that there must be moonlight, probably a full moon by the amount of light.

As soon as the man had tried the handle, he set to work. He had the screws off in no time and, with a little leverage, the bolt was free. The trouble was, if he pushed the door open, the bolt would fall to the ground and make a noise. Jake thought for a moment, then screwed one of the screws back in and pushed very gently. The door opened a bit, stuck and then jerked free, leaving the bolt dangling from its single screw. Jake held his breath again.

No one seemed to have heard the slight creak and tinkle. All was very still. Clutching his two loads, bending low and keeping close to the wall of the hut, he scurried out of the door and round to the back. Still no alarm. He could see the edge of the forest about 50 metres away and, by the glint of moonlight on water, he could see where it reached the river upstream of where they had landed. That was the spot to aim for; but whether to run, walk or crawl? He decided that crawling would take much too long; running was dangerous, as he might trip and make a noise; and so he set off walking slowly but steadily towards the darkness of the forest. He dare not look back and, as the distance increased between himself and the huts, he began to feel dreadfully exposed. At any moment he expected a shout or the sound of running feet — or a shot. The urge to run became stronger and stronger until at last he gave in to it and dashed into the shadows, where he stood stock still.

Now he turned and looked back. All was silent and, apart from a curl of smoke rising from one of the huts, there was no movement. The sentry must be inside or somewhere else. Thank goodness there were no dogs, thought Jake. He turned again and looked ahead into the darkness. As his eyes adjusted he could see that a path ran along the river bank and that it was lit up at intervals by shafts of moonlight. He set off briskly, trying not to think about snakes which might be lying across the track, or jaguars watching him from the side.

The night was full of sound now that he was among the trees. There were rhythmic whistles, grating noises and quite musical notes, all apparently competing with each other. He had no idea which were crickets and which tree frogs, but he had seen several television programmes about night life in the rainforest and so the sounds were almost familiar at first. Then, as he walked deeper into the darkness it all began to be more frightening and he had to force himself to think positively.

He had escaped. That must be good. Tomorrow there would be search parties out looking for him and, if he could reach them before the guerrillas caught him, he would be safe. He just had to get through the night. Luckily, the path was a good one and he was putting a lot of distance between himself and the camp. He strode on bravely.

The shot, when he heard it, was faint but unmistakable. Nothing in the rainforest sounds like a gun being fired, especially when it is repeated several times. He looked back but, being now well away from the camp, could see nothing. He hurried on, glancing over his shoulder every few moments. Sure enough, after about ten minutes he saw the flickering light of a torch through the trees. He must get off the path and hide. Plunging into the undergrowth, he felt himself plucked at and scratched by hooked vines. He reached the base of a huge tree and crept between two of the massive buttress roots supporting it. He felt, and was, completely invisible, but his breath was coming in frightened gasps. With a great effort he controlled it and listened intently.

He could now hear voices: Spanish, shouted and angry. He did not want to get caught as he had a nasty feeling that they would be much rougher than the last time; and his wrists were still quite sore from that experience. The torch light passed right over his head, lighting up the tree and showing him that it towered straight up above him to the sky, where he could see the silhouette of its bushy top against the stars. He hunched his neck down between his shoulder blades and kept his face turned towards the tree and away from the path, so that it wouldn't show up in the dark. He wondered if human eyes glowed in torch light like cats' eyes in a car's headlights and forced himself not to look round. This was not the time to find out.

The two men had stopped not far away and were talking. He heard them strike matches and light cigarettes. Although he could not understand the Spanish, he could pick out certain words, especially those which were repeated a lot. Among these were 'tigre', which sounded like tiger. Even he knew there weren't any tigers in South America, he thought. Perhaps they meant jaguars. The other word, on which there was a special sort of emphasis, was Maria. Jake suspected that must be the name of the girl with the penetrating eyes, their leader.

After a while, they carried on along the path. Jake decided he had better stay where he was, so as not to bump into them coming back. And, sure enough, after about an hour, they did come back, muttering together and running quite fast. As they headed back towards the camp he could see in the light of the torches they carried, that in their other hands they had guns. He heaved up his two bundles, checked that he had his hat and his knife and set off again in the opposite direction.

After a while he began to feel dreadfully tired. It had been a very long day and he simply couldn't keep going. Moreover, the path was beginning to fade out and he was starting to stumble over roots. Turning off again to the right, towards where the river ought to be, he found another buttress tree. Unwrapping his parcel, he allowed himself one boiled sweet, spread the ground sheet down, folded himself in the hammock and was almost instantly asleep.

6
The Rainforest

During the night, his deeply sleeping body was investigated by a myriad insects and animals. A continuous line of termites, across whose regular trail up and down the tree he lay, readjusted their route to climb on to his feet, trudge four abreast over the hammock and leave again from about the level of his shoulder. Fast moving ants dashed everywhere, investigated everything, tickled his hair and ears with their antennae but, as he lay still, saw no reason to bite him with their formidable pincers. A long green snake looped over the buttress root, paused testing the strange scent with its forked tongue, then slithered quickly and almost weightlessly across his legs. A coati-mundi, busily grubbing through the forest floor in search of insects, lifted its long sensitive nose as it approached the tree. Freezing in its tracks at the dangerous and unfamiliar smell of man, it shook itself, sneezed and hurried away.

The night was full of small noises and bustling activity, but Jake was aware of none of it; dead to the world in a deep, dreamless sleep.

He awoke with a start, feeling suddenly hot and uncomfortable. A shaft of sunlight had reached his hiding place, which faced east towards the little stream and rapidly warmed him. He pushed back the cotton hammock in which he was wrapped and sat up. There were some ants investigating the big bunch of bananas, but otherwise he seemed to have no visitors. He ate a couple of bananas for breakfast and began to think what he should do now. He knew he was invisible where he was from the path, sandwiched between the two great buttresses. It was tempting to spend the day there and wait to see what happened next. But they were sure to go on looking for him and if they came up the stream in a boat he would be seen. On the other hand, he had no idea where he was or in which direction he should head if he was to try and reach help.

The little stream seemed to run north/south, since the sun was rising across it and it flowed to his right. This meant that the camp of the guerrillas was to the south. East into the sun might mean the whole of the vast Amazon basin, an endless wilderness which he had glimpsed from the plane as they landed, stretching for thousands of miles towards the Atlantic. West lay either the Ucayali river, if they were that side of it, or the high Andes lying between him and the Pacific. He wasn't sure what lay north, but at least the path went that way and it would take him directly away from the camp. He decided to go north.

Gathering up his things, tying up the bundle securely, he crept to the edge of the path, looked carefully right and left, then stepped out onto it and began to trot north, the sun reassuringly low on his right. Soon he felt too hot to run and slowed to a steady walk. Now, for the first time since he had escaped, he had a chance to look around him.

The forest was surprisingly open. From the air and from the boat, as they headed towards the picnic, it had looked dense and impenetrable, a solid mass of vegetation. Deep inside it was open, almost like the woods of beech and oak near his home in England. Thinking of that he felt a sudden stab of homesickness. For a moment he ached physically to be safe with his mother and Philip. Then he thought to himself 'No. I must be brave. I am with Dad now and he wouldn't want me to be a wimp. I'm going to get out of here on my own.' He could imagine his father putting his hand on his shoulder and saying 'Well done!' and he resolved not to give up but to go on being sensible. After all, they had done the rainforests in school last term and he could remember his teacher, Mrs North, saying what a great place it was. Of course she had never actually been in one but she did seem to know a lot about it and there had been lots of interesting books with good pictures. He wished now that he had paid a little more attention.

One thing he did remember Mrs North saying was that most of the life was up in the canopy. He looked up. Far above him he could make out a sort of layer against the sky. The branches and leaves seemed to meet like interlocking fingers, leaving only a few cracks through which the light filtered. From that distant world came a steady hum, like listening to a bee hive. Now that he looked he caught glimpses of birds or butterflies flitting about. Or were they insects? It was hard to tell at that distance. Something much bigger was moving slowly along. He stopped in his tracks, his mouth open, as he realized that it was a black monkey swinging from branch to branch. It looked like a spider and seemed to have five legs. Could it be a spider monkey?

Tearing his eyes away from the distant creature — it almost made him giddy to see how high up it was — he let his eyes travel down through successive and ever thinner layers of canopy until they rested once more on the forest floor. Practically all the trees were either huge or tiny; it gave him a strange sensation when he noticed this, like a half dream he sometimes had when he was very tired and the shapes he saw behind closed eyes expanded and contracted dramatically. He remembered being told how young saplings waited for years and years if need be in the semi-darkness before shooting up towards the light when one of the forest giants eventually fell. These giants rose tall and straight into the sky, many supported by dramatic buttresses like the ones he had spent the night between. Some had lianas, creepers, trailing down them so that they looked as though they could be climbed. Most soared majestically up with smooth trunks, from which occasional strange lumps protruded. The forest floor itself was, in places, bare or covered only in dead leaves. Elsewhere weeds and shrubs grew, but mostly they were no thicker than at home. Where gullies or water courses crossed the path, these were usually dense with rushes and reeds.

In the bottom of these ditches there was sometimes water or mud, and in one of these Jake spotted the footprints of the two men who had overtaken him the night before. One had big boots

46

on with a distinctive pattern in the sole. The other wore narrower lightweight trainers like Jake's own. He began to watch out for these footprints and to take care to leave none of his own. After all, if he could recognize theirs it would not take much for one of them to recognize his.

After a while he noticed that there were no more footprints and he guessed that he had now gone further along the path than the men had run in the night. The path was becoming fainter and seemed to be leaving the stream, which he had not seen for some time. The sun was high overhead and this meant that he had no idea in which direction he was going. However, there was nothing else for it but to keep putting as much distance between himself and the guerrillas as possible.

The bunch of bananas began to feel heavy and was rather awkward to carry so, during the afternoon, he stopped to rest and ate a few, carefully burying the skins so that they didn't give him away. When the path seemed to divide later on he took the left fork, hoping that might lead him back towards the main river, but soon afterwards he realized that he was lost. All around him were tracks and he could no longer tell which was the one by which he had arrived. He felt a strong temptation to panic and start running, but he resisted it and stopped to think.

The only thing different now was that the sun had dropped in the sky, creating some shadows. Since he had set off heading north, he might as well continue in the same direction, he decided. This meant keeping the sun on his left now, as it would be setting in the west. For most of the day the forest had been much the same and, after his first look up into the canopy, he had kept his eyes on the ground ahead, watching out for roots and trying to follow the faint track. Now he realized that the vegetation was becoming thicker and he was having to push creepers and undergrowth to one side. He thought of turning back but the ground seemed to be sloping downhill ahead of him and he hoped that this might mean there was a river ahead. He had not had a drink for some time and he was feeling thirsty. Just when he thought it would be impossible to push any further forward, he caught a glimpse of sunlight on water ahead and a few moments later he burst out from the murk beneath the trees into broad daylight.

Spread out invitingly before him was the most delightful scene. A clear stream flowed between wide flat rocks, over a little waterfall and into a deep pool. There were no weeds and the water was so clear that he could see right down to the bottom and so be sure that he had it to himself. Hot and sweaty after two days and a night in the same clothes it was irresistible. Stripping off, he plunged in.

7

Alone

The feel of the water was wonderfully refreshing and it was exactly the right temperature. The rocks were hot from the sun and lying on them he was soon dry and warm again. Stretching out, he lay back and moved his clothes under his head as a pillow. They stank of mud and sweat and he did not like the idea of putting them on again like that. The only answer was to wash and dry them before the sun set.

Without soap all he could do was to squeeze and pummel everything, alternately dunking them in the stream and wringing them out. This was surprisingly successful, especially with the socks, which released lots of brown juice into the water.

While his clothes were drying on the warm rocks, Jake had time to sit and think what he should do next. He did not feel like going any further and he had found such a nice place that the temptation to stay there was overwhelming. Also, the forest which surrounded him on all sides was beginning to look gloomy and forbidding in the evening light. If he was going to camp there, the first thing to do was to decide where to sleep. The rocks were warm but would presumably get cold in the night and anyway he felt a bit exposed at the thought of sleeping right out in the open. On the other hand, the prospect of plunging back into the forest to find another buttress tree did not appeal either. Then he remembered the hammock. Of course!

He unwrapped his bundle and laid out all his possessions on the ground. The hammock was by far the largest single item and, apart from the ground sheet and the blanket, there was very little else. Just on the edge of the rocks beside the pool a twisted tree leant out over a sandy beach. After a couple of false starts, when he tried to tie the hammock's ends to branches which were much too close together, so that it hung steeply down and touched the ground, he found exactly the right limbs and secured the ropes firmly. He used the same knot he had had such trouble untying in the hut, thinking to himself that it would be useful if he could release it quickly in an emergency.

When he tried climbing into the hammock, he found that it sank to only a couple of feet above the ground, but this meant that he could spread out the ground sheet underneath and put all his things within easy reach. Suddenly he felt hungry and he scrambled out of the hammock and went over to where his clothes were laid out. They were almost dry but the sun was now sinking fast and, as he already knew happens in the tropics, it would soon be dark. Before washing his shirt he had emptied the pockets of all the rice he had crammed in them the evening before and put it in a small hollow in the rock, which made a perfect bowl. This he now ate. It was cold and rather greasy but he was so hungry he didn't care and convinced himself easily that it would not keep another day. With two more bananas inside him, followed by two of the sticky sweets left by the man who had brought his food and a long drink of cool river water, he felt much better.

As the sun sank behind the trees, it immediately became cooler and he put on all his clothes again. They did feel better for their wash even though they were still a bit damp in places. The world about him seemed to be becoming noisier with dusk. Flocks of green parrots went past shrieking stridently at each other. Their colourful feathers caught the last of the sun as they skimmed over the treetops. They were followed by much more dignified pairs of blue and yellow macaws, who just squawked and grunted at each other occasionally. One pair landed on two adjacent trees across the river and began to set up a frightful racket. At first Jake thought it must be because they had seen him and were shouting at him to go away; then he realized that it was nothing to do with him. They were clearly having a disagreement about where to roost. Each was determined that his or her tree was the best and would not give up and join the other. They were like an old married couple arguing the toss, both obstinate and rather bad tempered. At last one of them flew to the other and immediately the noise stopped as they perched close together side by side and nuzzled each other with their beaks.

Now he could spot more movement on the river. Everywhere he looked he glimpsed the flash of a wing as a bird dipped down for a last drink or something scurried through the undergrowth at the water's edge. Flying beetles and dragonflies hovered over the surface and there seemed to be a haze like mist there as well. It was not long before he found out what that was. A cloud of tiny insects surrounded his head and began to bite. Each one left a tiny red mark where it had drawn blood. They were quite painful, too, and he was soon slapping himself desperately, killing hundreds at each blow but having no effect on the numbers attacking him. Hurriedly he gathered up all his possessions, dumped them below the hammock and climbed in. Wrapped in the blanket, he was able to bury his head and escape the plague of insects, although it was hard to breathe and what he did breathe was smelly. It was also hot and stuffy but there was no alternative except to get back in the river and submerge.

Uncomfortable and unable to sleep, he had time to think. Once again, he longed for someone to talk to, someone to tell him what to do. It was tempting to think about going back, trying to retrace his steps, find the camp and hope that either help had arrived or the guerrillas had left. But he knew he mustn't do that. They would only catch him again and he would be worse off than before. There was nothing for it, really, but to go on. He would keep going in the same direction and hope to meet a road, a river or people eventually.

The insect plague lasted a couple of hours, by which time it was pitch dark. Now Jake was able to poke his head out of the blanket and breathe deeply the sweet night air. He also started to listen and what he heard was increasingly frightening. For a start there was a strange booming coming from far across the river. It was very deep and seemed to make the ground shake. He could not imagine what it could possibly be. Closer to home there were higher chirps and peeps, which sounded like bird-song but must, he supposed, be frogs. There were also the unmistakable croaks of frogs or toads, one of which sounded as though it was right below the hammock. It was loud, repetitive, seemed to be speaking directly to him and would not stop. He wished he had a torch so that he could shine it around. He also wished he had a fire, but that was out of the question as he had no matches. Even if he had, he decided that he would rather stay snug in his hammock than start walking around in the dark. All he could do was lie and listen. He began to find the singing and the chirping of all the night insects and amphibians quite pleasant and restful, so that he found himself beginning to doze off. The darkness was absolute and he felt secure wrapped in his blanket. Then he heard the first footstep.

He froze and sat up straight, making the hammock swing from side to side. Petrified, he held on to the sides, suddenly afraid that he would fall out. He listened harder than he had ever listened before. Then he heard another step ... and another. There could be no doubt about it. Someone ... or some thing was walking towards him. He heard the undergrowth rustle as it brushed past. He heard a twig snap. Silence for a moment, then it began again. He began to imagine something huge and, staring into the blackness, thought he could see an immense shape. An elephant? No, they didn't have elephants in South America. What then? And why didn't it move? Another sound of rustling leaves behind him made him turn his head sharply and nearly overbalance. It was all too much and he slid down into the middle of the hammock, curled up in a ball and pulled the blanket over his head. Nothing happened, but he couldn't sleep and instead lay tense, waiting.

After a long time he decided that he must be brave and have another look. He pulled the blanket back and sat up. To his amazement, it was light. Once again the moon had risen while his head was under the blanket and now it shone above the trees across the pool, its light reflected in the water. Now he could see almost everything, although there were still dark patches of shadow where anything might lurk. The big shape was a tree. There was no big animal standing near. When he heard another step he leaned out of the hammock to look at the spot the sound came from and he was just in time to glimpse a large lizard leap over a fallen branch and crash land on some dry leaves. With a sigh Jake rolled over and went straight to sleep.

8
Survival

The high pitched whine of a mosquito preparing to land on his exposed ear woke Jake as he instinctively slapped at it. They had bothered him occasionally during the night but he had barely surfaced from his dreams as he either swatted them or buried his face in the blanket.

He had never known such vivid dreams. All night he seemed to have been wrestling with dangers and demons, though the setting, strangely, had been the orchard at home. There was something huge and horrible trying to get into the house and he was trying to warn his mother. But the only noise he could make was a faint squeak and she couldn't hear him. He was trying to get out of his hammock, which was as usual hanging between the two apple trees, but for some reason he could not. Very faintly he could hear his mother's voice singing the Scottish lullaby with which she used to send him to sleep. When he opened his eyes they were full of tears.

It was daylight. There was a layer of mist over the water and dew on the leaves. With a sigh he stretched his arms above his head and prepared to face the day.

The forest was quiet now, except for some buzzing in the canopy far overhead where the first rays of the sun were already striking. He looked carefully round the pool, over the rocks and along the far bank. He seemed to be completely alone. Then his eye caught a shape in the sand close to where he lay and for a long time he was absolutely motionless as he stared at it. Very slowly, he pulled himself into a sitting position so that he could see better. He was not mistaken. It was a large paw print and there were more, leading in a line directly towards his hammock. Big cat! He knew a cat's paw print when he saw one. He had seen enough pictures of them and anyway this one was just like the tracks left by the farm cats at home . . . only much, much bigger. The men who had chased him had talked about tigers, but there are no tigers in South America any more than there are elephants. So it had to be a jaguar, the biggest New World cat and the only one which sometimes kills humans. But where was it now?

With a conscious effort he turned his head to look behind him and there, where the sand met the edge of the ground sheet, were more prints; only now they were heading away from him. The jaguar must have walked right under his hammock! Perhaps it was still watching him from the nearby undergrowth. He found he had been holding his breath and let it out in a long inaudible whistle. If the animal hadn't eaten him when he was asleep and defenceless, why would it want to do so now? Just for security he took out his Swiss Army knife and opened the largest blade. It didn't look much defence against a big cat but he felt better and, after holding it up so that it caught the first ray of sunlight filtering through the trees, he closed it again and shoved it back in his pocket.

'That'll show him I mean business,' he said to himself, and swung out of the hammock to land barefoot on the sand. He measured the size of his own footprint beside one of the jaguar's and found his was about twice as long. 'At least I've got bigger feet,' he thought.

Looking round his campsite, he was tempted again to stay there. 'After all,' he thought to himself, 'I should be fairly safe here as no one is likely to find me and it's much nicer than inside the dark and prickly jungle. On the other hand, I want someone, the right someone, to find me and he's not likely to come here. I could just sit here until I starved. And if Dad did fly over in a plane, how on earth would I attract his attention? I do wish I had a way of making a fire so that he might see the smoke.'

For a while he sat thinking, sure that there must be something he could do to light a fire without matches but not getting anywhere. Rubbing two sticks together seemed such an unlikely solution, but he decided that if nothing else occurred to him he would have a go later. Meanwhile the forest still looked forbidding and he hesitated to leave the friendly open sandbank and rocks. A movement on the surface of the pool caught his eye. Something was swimming across it. Standing up, he saw that it was a long brown snake moving fast, its head slightly raised above the water. It seemed to be heading straight for him and he froze as it reached the shore and, ignoring him completely, squirmed away across the warm sand at much the same speed as it had been swimming and vanished into the undergrowth. For the second time that morning Jake found himself letting his breath out in a whistle. He began to realize that perhaps he was not, as he had thought, the centre of attention for all the rest of the inhabitants. Provided he didn't interfere with them, they might leave him alone. The encounter helped him to make up his mind.

It was time to pack up and move on. Putting all thoughts of lurking predators aside, he packed up his few possessions inside the hammock, ate three of the last ten bananas, which were by now becoming rather mushy and overripe, put on his trainers and strode off. The morning sun was on his right, which meant that he was still heading north. Only now he was walking downstream. He paused for a moment to think about that. It couldn't still be the same river, he decided. Some time on the previous day, while he was lost and wandering away from the bank of his original river, he must have crossed a watershed so that this was a new stream. It must eventually lead to a bigger river and there he might find people. Or so he hoped.

At first, close to the river bank, he had to push his way through the bushes and once again he was scratched by thorns. Then, quite suddenly, it opened up, the trees became much bigger and there was even something that looked like a path for him to follow. Fortunately, it seemed to be running parallel to the river, as he was anxious not to lose contact with that.

As he walked, he went on worrying about how to make a fire. He had no idea which sort of sticks to use and he very much doubted if any old twigs would ever catch alight, however hard he rubbed them together. There must have been something useful he had learned in chemistry. Mr Reilly, the science teacher, was always saying that you could do almost anything if you knew how and he was sure that there had been a discussion about fire one day in class. There were various things one could do with chemicals, he remembered, only he couldn't remember what, and anyway he didn't have any chemicals. The floor of the forest was either bare earth or covered in creeping plants: they were no help. There was another way, he was sure.

Ahead of him a massive tree had crashed to the ground quite recently, taking several other, smaller trees with it and creating a large clearing. Suddenly, he was in bright sunlight and within a few paces he was sweltering in the heat. 'I'm almost burning,' he thought. 'That's funny, when I'm thinking about fire all the time,' and something began to niggle at a corner of his mind. But all thought was abruptly interrupted when he spotted a fat speckled snake curled up right on the path in front of him. Unlike the long thin one in the water, this one looked dangerous and indeed as he stopped dead just short of it he saw that its head was up and that it was looking at him. For a long moment they stared at each other without moving. Then Jake began to suspect that the snake could not actually see him, as it was waving its head very slowly from side to side and seemed to be testing the air with its tongue. He knew that this was how snakes smelled and held his breath. 'I'm getting quite good at doing that,' he thought.

Very very slowly, he began to back away. When he

stepped backwards onto a stick and it cracked under his foot, the snake made a sudden move and stretched out towards him. Now it was casting about quite urgently as though wanting to attack him and he had a nasty feeling it was getting closer. Rather than wait for it to reach him, he continued to walk backwards — he had decided not to take his eyes off it — until he felt that he was well out of striking range. Leaving the path, he headed off at right angles to make a wide detour. Now he could take no precautions against disturbing another snake, but he was so anxious to avoid this one that he simply pushed his way unheeding through the undergrowth. As a result he was again scratched, his shirt torn and he was sweating hard by the time he regained the path. As he left the clearing and entered the dark forest again he kept glancing over his shoulder, imagining that the snake was following him.

After a while his heart stopped pounding and he began to walk more slowly. Sitting on a fallen log he had a rest and ate the last of the bananas. He was going to have to get some more food soon or else he was going to be hungry. Deep in thought, he set off again along the path.

For several hours he strode on, thinking deeply while at the same time being careful to keep a sharp eye on where he was stepping so as not to run into any more unexpected hazards. Once, something made him stop suddenly and look up from the ground, to which his eyes were normally glued. Just ahead of him and at about the level of his hat was a strange sort of basket hanging above the path. For a moment he thought it must be something man-made, perhaps an Indian offering to some spirit. Then he saw that it was made of thin wafers of material which seemed to be glued together to make a shape a bit like a pineapple. It reminded him of a wasps' nest he had once seen and, sure enough, as he watched an orange and black insect emerged from a hole in the side and flew away. But this was no wasp. It was about three times as big as any wasp he had ever seen and had long trailing legs. A hornet of some sort, he thought, and it looked as though it could deliver a really vicious sting. Several more came out and flew off in the same direction, luckily away from him. Had he not looked up when he did, he would have crashed into the nest and the result of that did not bear thinking about. With a shiver, he detoured around the hornets' nest and continued on his way.

By mid afternoon, his legs were beginning to ache and it was with a great sense of relief that he glimpsed the river again and decided to make his way to it and stop. As he burst out of the shade into the bright sunlight, he had to screw his eyes up against the glare and the heat of the sun's direct rays hit him. Immediately the thoughts which had been churning about in his head all day fell into place and he knew how he was going to make a fire. At the same moment he heard the sound of an aeroplane engine.

Frantically, he began to gather a little heap of the driest leaves and little twigs he could find. When they were piled up neatly and looked like a miniature bonfire, he took out his Swiss Army knife and opened out the tiny magnifying glass. Focusing the rays of the sun through it, he directed the little spot of bright light at the driest leaf in the pile.

The plane seemed to be circling and had not yet passed overhead but he dare not look up, concentrating instead on keeping his hand steady and the hot spot in one place. He could see the centre of the leaf beginning to crinkle and smoulder. A minute plume of smoke began to ascend from the leaf, but still no flame. The buzz of the plane became louder and he had to look up. Sure enough, there it was, high in the blue sky above, a silver single-engined aircraft and he knew that his father was in it. Despairingly, he abandoned the pathetic little column of smoke, which would not be visible from more than a few paces, stood up and began to wave as hard as he could. He took out his handkerchief and waved that, but he knew as he did so that it was hopeless. There was no way anyone, however hard they were looking and however much they might to trying to see him, could spot anything as small and insignificant as he knew himself to be in that vast expanse of greenery. To his shame, tears streamed down his face as he shouted 'Dad!' and reached his arms out towards the plane as it passed out of sight over the trees. Then it was gone and the sound was fading in the distance. Jake sat and wept tears of misery and frustration, his face buried in his hands.

9
Fire

For a while he sat motionless in his misery, and around him the creatures of the forest seemed to share his grief so that there was no sound to be heard. When he looked up, the devastating sense of loneliness and isolation which that brief glimpse of the plane, in which he was convinced his father had been searching for him, had given him was replaced by a peculiar feeling that he was not alone but was part of the life of the forest. It was as though the realization that he was unlikely to be rescued soon brought with it an acceptance of the need to come to terms with his surroundings. He found himself breathing in and out deeply several times, almost as though he were preparing for a race. Quite deliberately, he made himself calm down and stop feeling sorry for himself. 'You're on your own now, Jake old man,' he said aloud. 'No one else is going to help you, so you'd better get on with looking after yourself.' He felt better after that, almost as if he really had been speaking to someone. The loneliness left him and he had a momentary but distinct impression that there were friends around him, willing him on.

Slowly he stood up, stripped off his shirt and

washed his face in the river. Looking around for the first time, he saw that he had struck the river at another good camp site. There were wide, flat rocks next to a much deeper pool, which looked as though it ought to have fish in it. With a sigh he turned back to the little bonfire.

There was no smoke any more and the leaves were quite cold. Focusing the sun's rays through the lens again, he was soon able to generate enough heat for another leaf to start smouldering but it was some time before he learnt the trick of blowing gently while placing other dry scraps next to the hot spot. At last a leaf burst into flame and then, by carefully adding to that fragile start, he soon had a proper fire going.

As the now thick column of smoke rose straight up into the still air above the canopy of trees, he strained his ears in the hope of catching the faintest sound of a distant plane. Nothing. Well, at least he had proved that he could do it and now he had a fire. What use was that if not to summon help? He didn't need the heat, though that might be welcome later when darkness fell, and it would be nice to have the comfort of a fire in the night. He could feel quite pleased with himself, he supposed, but there must be more he could do with a fire now he had made one. Of course! He could cook on it! That is, if he had anything to cook.

Sitting down, he spread out his hammock and unwrapped all his possessions. There was not much food left. The bananas were all gone and so was the rice. Ten boiled sweets and five pieces of chewing gum didn't look much. Then he remembered the raisins in his hat. He opened the pocket and spilled them out. It was tempting to eat them but they had a higher purpose. From the other side of the hat band he extracted the fishing line and hooks which Jaime had given him at his house. That all seemed such a long time ago.

Luckily, Jake had been taught by his father, on the fishing trip to Scotland, how to tie a hook onto a line with a fisherman's knot. Choosing a medium-sized hook, he carefully fixed a raisin on it; then he realized that he had no rod. Laying everything down, he walked to the bank and looked around for a nice straight pole. He found one that looked perfect, but it was much too hard to break. The Swiss Army knife had a little saw on it, which he had always wanted to use. Now was the time. It was slow but effective and eventually, after a bit of trimming, he had a fine two metre rod. Of course, there were no rings along it to carry the line and so he drilled a small hole near the tip with the marlin spike in the penknife. He threaded the line through and at last he was ready. He plopped the raisin well out into the pool.

At first nothing happened and he began to worry that perhaps there was nothing there. Then he felt a gentle tug. He had the end of the line wrapped around his hand at the thick end of the rod so that he could feel what was going on with his other hand on the line. There were several more little tugs – and then nothing. He pulled the line out of the water to see a bare hook. Whatever it was had just eaten the raisin without getting hooked. He put another raisin on and tried again.

This time, at the first tug he jerked the tip of the rod up and, sure enough, there was a little catfish dangling on the end. It looked rather sweet with its long whiskers as he took hold of it, but he nerved himself to do the necessary and shoved the hook deep into its body before throwing it back in.

Almost at once, there was a strong pull on the line and he dragged a big snapping piranha up onto the rock where it leapt about alarmingly, snapping its teeth. Keeping well clear of it, Jake decided not to try and attack it with his small knife. The chances of losing a finger looked too great. Instead, he put down the rod and ran to the edge of the river where he found a big hardwood stick. With this he hit the piranha hard on the head and only when it lay still did he start gingerly trying to cut its head off with the biggest blade on the knife. At once the fish came to life again and started snapping furiously. By placing the stick across its body and standing on it, he was able to keep it still long enough to get started but, to his horror, the jaws went on snapping for some time after he had removed the head. However, he now had another piece of bait well attached to the hook and this he cast back into the water.

In no time he had the bodies of four plump piranha lying on the rock attracting flies. It was time to cook them, and he suddenly realized that he was very hungry. First he carefully removed his hook from the last fish head, using the special tool on his knife for this purpose and wedging a piece of wood between the jaws so that they could not bite him. The gadget was like a blunt knife but with a serrated edge for scaling fish and a notch in the end, which fitted under the hook to prise it out. Along the side was a ruler marked out in centimetres and inches and for fun he measured the biggest of the piranha with it. Gingerly putting the head back with the body, he found that it was just over 25 centimetres, or 10 inches long. Then he coiled the line up and put it back in his hat. Now it was time to clean the fish. This was another rather unpleasant chore which his father had made him do with each of the fish he had caught in Scotland and so it did not take him long. Putting the point of the sharpest blade into each fish's vent, he sliced forward up its belly so that it opened up and the insides spilled out. The nasty bit was having to run a finger up the inside of the spine so as to separate the intestines from the body, but they came away easily enough, leaving the fish clean and ready to cook.

The guts he threw back into the pool without thinking. Immediately the water started to boil around them as the waiting cannibal fish set about their cousins' insides. Jake watched this thoughtfully and decided not to dive in and swim across the pool to cool off, as he had been planning to do. Instead, he washed the fish slime off his hands in a safe and warm little pool in the rock.

The fire had died down, leaving good hot embers. Pushing a green stick right through each of the fish, he laid them on the fire. At once, the skin started to crinkle and peel off revealing the tender white flesh beneath. By the time he had turned each fish over and grilled the other side, Jake's mouth was watering and he burnt his fingers in his hurry to pick the first one up and start eating. There was plenty of meat to fill him up satisfactorily and, once he had hung his hammock, he lay stretched out in it feeling pretty good and quite pleased with himself. It would all make an amazing story to tell his school friends when he got home. Home. That seemed an awfully long way away and he found himself becoming sad again.

In order to take his mind off his problems, he decided to explore his surroundings before settling down for the night. The river bank looked quite easy to walk along and so he set off downstream.

The sun was now low and it was becoming cooler. The evening activity of parrot flights and noisy calls from all sides was building up and there was lots of interest going on. Clouds of yellow butterflies rose from around his feet, apparently unafraid as they fluttered off to a new spot. When he stopped to pee, he was amused to notice that they returned to settle on the damp patch he had made on the sand.

'Must be something there they like,' he said to himself out loud. The sound of his voice surprised him. He realized that he had not heard a word spoken since he had last listened to the guerrillas muttering about 'tigres' as they passed his hiding place two days before. Well, he rather liked the sound of a human voice and so he decided to talk to himself for comfort and companionship. People might think him mad but if he ever met people again he wouldn't mind.

Before he could think of anything else to say to himself, he came round a bend in the river and stopped dead. Another pool lay ahead but this one had a wide sandy beach and on it were some very strange animals. They looked like giant rabbits, only much, much bigger. The adults were well over a metre long and seemed fat, being almost a metre around the middle. They had funny square faces with a droopy upper lip split down the middle, giving them a silly superior expression. He had seen a wildlife film once about capybaras, the biggest rodents in the world, and he gasped as he recognized them. He remembered that the commentator had said that they were perfectly harmless.

He hid behind a big boulder and watched, fascinated, as the family played together at the water's edge. They seemed as much at home in the water as out of it and the little babies were clearly enjoying the fun. They plunged in and out, chasing each other both on the sand and under water, giving little grunts of pleasure. Suddenly, they all stopped and listened, some sitting up comically on their hind legs, so that Jake wanted to laugh. Then he heard, and smelled, whatever it was that had scared them. Something was approaching through the forest on the same bank as they all were. It sounded like the rumble of distant thunder and there was an acrid smell carried ahead of it on the evening breeze.

The capybaras plunged as one into the river and vanished under the water without surfacing again. Jake crouched down lower behind his rock as whatever it was reached the edge of the forest and paused. For a moment there was silence, then out into the open rushed a herd of small black pigs. Jake had been quite scared wondering what on earth could have been coming and he was so relieved that he laughed out loud. At once, all the pigs stopped dead, cocked their heads on one side and tested the air with their snouts. They looked so funny that he laughed again and stepped out into the open. He was not afraid of pigs. He had learnt all about them from Mr Thomas, the neighbouring farmer at home, who kept pigs and was an expert on the subject. Jake had often gone over to feed them. They liked to have their backs scratched.

Instead of running away, as he had expected, they turned to look at him and there was something about the way they looked that made him feel suddenly cold. Something Mr Thomas had told him sprang into his mind: how not all pigs were as friendly as his, how the most feared and dangerous animals in the Brazilian rainforest were not jaguars or snakes but the local sort of pig which hunted in large herds killing and eating anything that got in their way. He even remembered their name: the white-lipped peccary.

As one, they began to move towards him; a terrible clacking sound came from them and he realized they were gnashing their teeth as they gathered speed.

10
Pain

For a horrified moment Jake stared at the charging horde. There must have been a hundred of the brutes, their heads down, grunting, chomping and squealing as they trotted at him. There could be no question but that they intended attacking him. He had never been attacked by an animal before. All those he had known had been friendly or at least, like Mr Thomas's cows, indifferent. These meant business and it was time to get away from them. But where?

The speed with which they were crossing the sand indicated that they would go fairly fast even over the rocks when they reached them. Should he jump into the river and swim across to the other side? What if they could swim as fast as they ran? And anyway he was just downstream of where all those piranha had been getting so excited about the entrails and they might still be hungry. A tree! That was the best bet, but which one? Many, he had noticed, had sharp spines or hooked thorns all the way up their trunks and it had occurred to him that they were designed specifically to stop people climbing them.

He turned to run, then noticed a large tree leaning out over the river, from which hung several creepers. He had had to duck under these as he walked down the river shore and they looked climbable. Running fast, he reached them just as he heard the pigs clattering over the rocks with their sharp little hooves.

'They'll be clattering over me soon if this doesn't work,' he said as he leapt at the strongest looking creeper and began to pull himself up hand over hand. Fear gave him strength and he was soon able to haul himself into a fork of the main tree. Below him was a black crowd of animals tearing at the hanging creepers and rooting furiously at the ground. The smell he had first noticed faintly on the evening air before they emerged from the forest was now strong and pungent, wafting up to him like an awful message. Some of the creatures had spotted him and were peering up at him with their angry little eyes.

Leaning around the trunk, he looked down to see what happened at the base of the tree. His tree had, at some time, fallen over and it had only been prevented from crashing into the river by the fork of another tree, in which it was now neatly lodged. Below that, the main trunk joined its own exposed roots, which stuck up in the air above a crater in the ground from which they had been wrenched when the tree fell. Many of the pigs were now rootling busily in the exposed soil and, to his horror, Jake noticed that some of them were clambering from there over the main trunk itself. It had not dawned on them yet that by following the trunk they could reach him fairly easily as the slope was not too steep and the tree was wide enough to run up.

Once they started it would be hard to stop them and if he was dislodged from his present perch he would fall to the ground to be torn apart in no time. He would have to do something to prevent them climbing the tree and the obvious defensive position was where the main trunk lay in the fork. There they would only be able to come at him one at a time and he would have something to hold on to.

Reluctantly, he clambered out of his safe nest and crawled out on to the trunk. Immediately all the pigs stopped what they were doing and looked up at him. They seemed to have a single mind, like a flock of birds, and it was clear to Jake that it was focused on him and it was not friendly.

As soon as he started crawling down towards the fork they started to scramble onto the bottom of the trunk and one or two of the braver ones began to take tentative steps up it. It took all his determination to keep going, heading straight towards his enemies, who were climbing towards him, but he felt sure that it was right for him to go on the attack.

Among the dead wood caught in the fork was a strong pole, like a larger version of his fishing rod, and this he was able to prise loose as soon as he reached it. While waiting for the first pig to venture as far as the fork he whittled the end into a sharp point and then thrust it through the gap.

His adversaries were disorganized. As soon as one got a good footing on the trunk and was about to set off up it, another would leap on and dislodge it. He was relieved to see that they did not seem to have very good balance. However, what was disturbing was the way they appeared to work things out and, eventually, co-operate. It was almost as though they were being directed by a leader. Indeed, there was one of their number much bigger than all the rest. Greyer and hairier than the others, he had great tusks showing at the corners of his snout and he was doing a lot of bullying and biting around the foot of the tree. Now there was only one animal on the trunk and it was climbing steadily up towards the fork. Once it was well on the way another leapt on to follow.

Jake waited until the ugly snuffling creature was almost on him before he thrust his spear at it with a sudden movement. Surprised, the pig jumped sideways and, without even being struck, fell squealing to the ground where it was immediately set on by the rest.

The next one, however, had not been dislodged and now came on more carefully. This time Jake thrust too early and only just had time to draw the spear back and thrust again as his opponent reached the fork. He struck the animal in the side and the sharpened point went in. Pushing with all his strength while the pig's trotters scrabbled vainly for a secure foothold, he gradually forced it to the edge and over; then he had his work cut out hanging on to the spear so that it was not wrenched from his grasp as the animal fell.

There was now a pause while his enemies seemed to regroup and make a plan. He felt the tree shake as they began to undermine its base, but he felt fairly sure that, with it so firmly wedged in the other tree, they would not be successful in bringing it down. While waiting, he resharpened the point of his spear, which had been broken off in the last combat.

Suddenly, they were coming at him thick and fast; rushing up the trunk and seeming not to care about staying on but more intent on leaping on him before he could push them off. Fortunately, this was not so difficult to do and he almost began to enjoy himself, except that it was all so frightening. As they jostled for position, he remembered a great poem he had learnt at school about the Roman Centurion Horatius holding a bridge over the River Tiber and he began to quote a bit which came back to him.

'Was none who would be foremost
To lead such dire attack;
But those behind cried "Forward!"
And those before cried "Back!" '

As he tired, he remembered that Horatius had had two companions to help him — and also that at the end of the poem he had died. He was panting from the effort now as he waited for the next attack. There was sweat in his eyes and it took him a moment to see what was coming. It was the big brute, on his own and looking as though he meant business. He walked so surely along the trunk and with such grim confidence that Jake was suddenly sure that he would not be able to push him off, as he had managed to do with such relative ease to the others. It was time for desperate measures.

The monster reached the fork and he let it begin to force its way through before, taking careful aim, he jabbed it in the eye with all his strength. With a terrible roar it reared up on its hind legs and for a moment he thought it was going to crash down on him and take him with it. Letting go of the spear, he began to scramble away and up the trunk. Turning, he looked back to see the huge creature struggling in the fork, where it appeared to be jammed, the spear sticking out of its eye, from which blood was now spurting. Shaking its head desperately from side to side in its efforts to dislodge the spear, it suddenly lost its footing and hurtled down on to the herd below. The noise was now deafening as all those who had previously acknowledged it as their master now set upon it and, maddened by the taste of blood began to tear it apart. Unable to watch, Jake climbed carefully up the trunk as far as he could go, wedged himself in another fork and waited.

It looked as though the rest of the herd might have been discouraged from further attempts to reach him, but they did not go away and seemed to be settling down for the night, which was now fast approaching. All he could do was to make himself as comfortable as possible and wait until the moon rose.

He had no weapon now and so he took out his knife, opened the big blade and laid it on the branch beside him. If they did try to creep up on him in the dark, he would be ready, he thought. It was his last conscious thought for some time. Exhausted by all the fighting and with nothing to look at as darkness had fallen with the suddenness of the tropics, he fell asleep.

Anyone who has tried sleeping in the fork of a tree will know that it makes for a restless night, much troubled with dreams. Had Jake not been so tired he would probably have stayed awake, easing his cramped limbs and listening for danger.

Instead, he dropped into a deep sleep and only halfway through the night did the dreams come.

He was at home again, and again something was terribly wrong. All the animals from Mr Thomas's farm had invaded the orchard and they were causing dreadful damage. The pigs were rootling in the flowerbeds, the cows were munching on the shrubs, the chickens and geese were scrabbling through the trees. His mother would be furious and would try in a minute to drive them out but she mustn't because they were dangerous. They weren't really animals at all but monsters in disguise and he must tell her, only she would never believe him. Frantically he thrashed about trying to get out of the hammock, which seemed to have become entangled round him, until suddenly he was free and falling. And falling . . .

11
Delirium

He landed with a terrible crash which both woke him up and knocked him out. So it was that when he came round some time later, as the first faint light of dawn was making silhouettes of the trees, he remembered falling. He did not remember the pain which now flooded over him and made him groan. The sound of his own voice reminded him of the pigs and he wondered why he had not been eaten by them. Cautiously opening his eyes, he looked across the nearby ground and saw no shapes moving about.

'I suppose they've pushed off,' he said, and felt better for saying it.

However, when he tried to sit up the pain washed over him again and he lay back to wait until it was light enough to see what was wrong with him. Most of the pain was in his left arm, which hurt like anything. He wondered if it was broken. This made him wonder if anything else was broken and he wiggled his toes as that was what people were always told to do in hospital stories on TV. They seemed all right.

After a while, he began to feel himself all over, very cautiously. Apart from a few bumps and bruises, there seemed to be no serious damage except for his arm and this was remarkable, he realized, when he looked up and saw how far he had fallen from the tree. Luckily, he had landed on a patch of sand and it was probably something on the way down which had caught his arm. With a certain amount of reluctance, as he was afraid of what he would see, he began to examine it. The first thing he saw was that there was blood; quite a lot of it. The whole of that side of his shirt was drenched in it and it was coming from his upper arm. He didn't want to look but knew he had to. Easing off his shirt, which made him groan again, he looked. It was not a pretty sight. There was a deep gash in the muscle out of which blood was oozing and the whole of his arm was grazed and scratched. Funnily enough, now that he had seen the extent of his wounds, they did not hurt quite as much.

Getting to his feet rather unsteadily, he started to make his way back to his camp, trailing his bloody shirt behind him. Then he remembered his knife and returned to look for it. He hoped it was not still up in the fork as he did not feel up to climbing all the way there again. A spot of bright red, much brighter than the place where his blood had soaked into the sand, showed where the knife had dropped blade first and buried itself up to the hilt. Gratefully, he folded the blade away and shoved it in his pocket.

Back at the camp it was tempting simply to flop into the hammock and sleep again, but he knew that he must treat his wound. He had seen too many Westerns not to have learned that it was fatal to leave the bullet in or fail to clean a wound. And so he squatted at the water's edge and washed it as well as he could. Then he scrubbed his handkerchief as clean as he could make it, tied it tightly around his bicep, washed his shirt and spread it out on a rock to dry. Only then did he allow himself the luxury of a boiled sweet and a sleep in the hammock.

He slept for most of the day, only getting up in the afternoon to catch some more piranha and light a fire to cook them on. He ate some and wrapped the rest in some large leaves for the next day, as he had decided that he must force himself to move on in the morning. The flies were troublesome as he lay in the hammock, followed by the evening biting bugs — interestingly, they had not bothered him up in the tree and he supposed that they must stay close to the ground. Later there were mosquitoes to disturb his sleep so that he awoke feeling feverish and unrested.

His arm throbbed. His handkerchief was stuck to the wound so that he chose not to have a look at it and break the scab. At least it was not bleeding any more. Packing up his things was much more effort than usual and when he started walking he felt tired almost before he had begun. But he made himself go on and trudged wearily along through the heat of the day, which seemed hotter than usual although the forest was still as deep and dark as ever.

By evening he was feeling dreadful and he barely had the energy to sling his hammock and crawl into it. The river was nowhere in sight and he was thirsty but he managed to chew up some of the cold fish and suck one of the remaining sweets before dropping into another troubled sleep.

The next morning he automatically packed up and struggled on again but he hardly knew what he was doing and soon he became delirious, talking rubbish to himself, wandering wherever any sort of path appeared to lead and only occasionally having lucid moments. Now the forest was full of people. He recognized his friend Keith, plodding patiently along driving a herd of cows in to milking. But when he called to him and he turned his face, it was Manolo's wizened features that looked at him and the cows were really huge black pigs with slavering jaws. Trying to run away, he saw that the undergrowth was full of nightmarish faces grinning at him. He could hear voices and cackling laughter. He ran, stumbled, fell and lay still. After a while he crawled to his feet and stumbled automatically on and on through a day which passed as a dream. Occasionally, he had lucid moments when he looked around, saw no faces, just an open, dark forest and the sun far overhead above the canopy creating long, dazzling shafts of light. During one of these moments of clarity, he noticed that the ground dropped away in one direction and, after scrambling through thick undergrowth with great difficulty, eventually reached a stream again but whether it was the same one he had no way of knowing. Desperately thirsty by now, he drank his fill, then splashed water over his fevered head.

His arm hurt like anything and he decided that he must have a look at the wound. Washing off his handkerchief, which had become caked on to his arm, he examined the cut and was shocked to see that it was red and puffy around the edges while the inside appeared white. Peering closer, he saw that the white part seemed to be moving. Feeling a bit better after his wash, he opened the magnifying glass on his knife in order to have a closer look. He could scarcely believe what he saw. The inside of his wound was crawling with tiny maggots!

How had they got there, he wondered? The flies which had settled on him and crawled all over his bloodstained handkerchief must have laid their eggs in the wound and these had hatched. Disgusted, he tried to pick them out, but he could not get hold of them. Eventually he nerved himself to use a bunch of grass to scrape out the inside of the cut and remove all maggots. It hurt abominably and he screamed aloud as he did it, but something told him that if he didn't do it now the pain would get worse and he would never be able to. Shaking from the pain and the horror, he bound the wound up again in the rinsed-out handkerchief, strung up his hammock and collapsed into it.

The next few days passed in a blur. He couldn't remember much about them afterwards, even whether he had stayed in the same place or travelled on. There had been more lucid moments, he knew. He had a clear recollection of a fruit tree of some sort which swarmed with birds and monkeys and where he had pushed and shoved among them to get his share. There had been a time when he had stared for ages at a footprint in the sand, wondering who it belonged to and trying desperately to work out whether he was dreaming, or if it was his own or somebody else's. And there had definitely been a moment when he had lain and watched a tapir drinking from the river before disporting in the water like an elephant, pushing its short trunk above the surface. Much later, he knew that that could not have been a dream, when he saw one doing exactly the same thing in a zoo.

Most of the time, however, he was delirious or asleep or unconscious and gradually he slipped into a coma from which he would never awake without help.

12
Indians

Jake's last conscious thought before he sank into oblivion had been that he could bear the pain of his throbbing arm no more. His first thought as he began to regain consciousness was that the pain had gone. He was lying in the luxurious comfort of a hammock and he could feel nothing. Cautiously he moved his right hand across to his left bicep. The wound was there all right but it didn't hurt any more. He kept his eyes closed and began to listen to the sounds around him. The forest seemed much quieter than it had before and he wondered what time of day it was. There were none of the noisy calls, hoots, buzzes, rasps and screeches with which he had become so familiar. Instead there was only a distant regular thumping and a sound like the low murmuring of voices.

Opening his eyes at last, he noticed at once that, although it was dark, he could see the sky above his head and it seemed to be made of some sort of woven thatch. He turned and there was a fire nearby. He could not remember lighting one. Then he saw a figure rise to put another stick on the fire and it dawned on him that he was no longer beside the river. He was too tired to feel shocked or frightened by whatever had happened to him and whatever was going to happen next. It was just so good not to be in pain, not to be frightened, not to be alone.

His arm had been wrapped in some sweet-smelling leaves and when he touched it there was still no pain. Wherever he was he seemed to be in good hands and so for a time he slept again.

The old Indian leaning over him had skin on his face like wrinkled parchment, a mouth full of smoke, which he released into Jake's face at precisely the moment when he looked up for the second time that day, and eyes so deep and dark and sunken that they were almost invisible. Strangely, the smoke did not make Jake cough but instead induced a sense of well-being.

'Hello,' he said, but the old Indian only looked at him solemnly, touched him lightly on the forehead and left.

Some time later a girl brought him some warm soup in a small wooden bowl. She helped him to drink straight from the bowl, holding his head forward so that he did not spill any. Only after she left did he realize that she had been wearing no clothes. Somehow her nakedness had seemed perfectly natural and not at all embarrassing. And besides, her body was beautifully decorated with delicate lines of red and black paint, there were fresh white flowers woven into arm bands and anklets, and she had a string of blue beads around her neck.

He checked to see if he had any clothes on and found that his had been removed. They hung from a pole beside him, within reach. He was relieved to be able to feel the solid bulge of his knife still in his trouser pocket. Someone had washed him and his body felt clean and fresh, but he blushed to think he had been so helpless. There was no doubt that he was with Indians, inside one of their thatched houses. He supposed they must have found him and carried him back with them but, try as he might, he could remember none of it. Still, they seemed kind and friendly and there didn't seem to be anything to worry about. He lay and dozed, watching life go on around him. There were tall poles reaching up into the darkness of the roof and he could see the light from several fires. People moved around in the half darkness from time to time, but no one bothered him.

Later, he felt strong enough to climb out of the hammock, pull on his trousers and totter very slowly towards the fire. There was a sore place in the sole of one of his feet which made him limp and he stopped to see if there was a thorn there but could find nothing. A group of Indians were squatting around a steaming bowl which had clearly just been lifted from the embers. In it were small pieces of meat and larger lumps of what looked like banana but which he recognized as plantain, the vegetable variety. The others made room for him exactly as though he were a member of their family and handed him a tin spoon. He noticed that most of them were using small wooden gourds to eat and understood that they realized he might find that difficult and were being kind. The stew was good and he ate quite a lot.

The pot on the fire was made of metal like his spoon but blackened with age. Almost everything else seemed to have been made by the Indians themselves. There were some beautifully decorated clay pots, woven fans for encouraging the fire to heat up when the pot was put back on it, baskets of various sizes and shapes and several hammocks suspended between poles supporting the roof. The last were made of what looked like the same material as the baskets and some of the Indians were sitting in them as they ate. There were two old women, a mother with a baby at her breast, the old man whom he had first seen on waking and the young girl.

He could now see that they were in a large thatched building shared by several families. Two or three other groups were gathered about fires, eating, and there were some other hearths with hammocks round them. With everyone at home there would have been about forty people in the house. The smoke from all the fires rose to the roof and filtered out through the thatch, leaving the rafters black. It was pleasantly cool inside and there were no insects.

Although he felt conspicuous and different, no one paid him any attention, except once or twice to offer him something from the pot and so, when he had had enough, he went back to his hammock and slept.

He woke to find that the girl had brought him some more soup. His bare foot, the one with the sore place, was outside the hammock and itching, so he leant over to scratch it before taking the soup. The girl stayed with him as he drank the soup, gazing at him without embarrassment from wide, almond-shaped eyes. When he had finished, she put the empty gourd down and picked up his foot, looking closely at the sore spot. Around her neck she had a

87

sharpened piece of bone hanging from a thin cord. This she now took off and with it she began to probe Jake's foot. He looked closely as she did so and could now see a small spot on the sole. Very carefully, so that he could barely feel it, she removed the skin around the spot, exposing something underneath which wriggled. Carefully, she impaled this on the end of the bone and pulled it out. It was a little maggot, smaller than those which had appeared in his wound. Several more turned up in his feet, but from then on he was able to deal with them himself, using the tweezers on his knife. Without the girl's help, he would never have guessed that there was anything beneath the faint mark on his foot.

Later, he needed to go outside and, ducking through the low entrance, emerged into the bright evening sunlight.

The house was built close to the edge of a larger river than the one he had been following, but not as big as the main Ucayali on which Jaime's house lay. It looked from the outside like a huge upside down basket, the thatch coming right down to the ground all round. There was an open area of bare earth all around with another, smaller building on the far side. Beyond that were some cultivated plots. Beyond, and on all sides except the river, rose the high wall of the forest.

Hearing children's voices, he walked down to the river. From the high bank he looked down and across a wide area of rocks and pools, in one of which half a dozen naked children were splashing each other and playing noisy games. Just below him, the mother from his hearth was tenderly washing her baby and far across the river a man was casting a net out into the main stream so that it landed like a parachute. It was a scene of perfect tranquillity and harmony. He could hardly believe that it was not all a dream after the misery of the last few days. He tried to remember what had happened and a few images came back to him but most of it was a blur of pain and misery. He assumed that he must have been found by the Indians and carried back to their home, but he could remember none of that.

There was a shout from the big house and he looked round in time to see someone walk out of the forest. It was a strong young man with a bow and arrows in one hand and a strange hairy animal draped over his shoulder. Jake walked over to see what it was and came face to face with the man. Without appearing to look at him, he flung the animal down on the ground outside the entrance and disappeared inside.

'How rude!' thought Jake. He noticed that no one else greeted the hunter or commented on his catch. Carefully turning the animal over with his foot, in case it was still alive, he tried to work out what it was. It had long hair with black and grey stripes along its body, ending in a huge bushy tail and it was a most peculiar shape. It seemed much bigger in the front than the back, with dangerous looking claws on its front feet and an extraordinary long, thin head which ended in an even longer nose. As he gazed and wondered, the children came running up laughing and shouting. They, too, ignored him at first and started feeling the animal, patting its body and stretching out the big tail. One little boy put his hand in its mouth and pulled out an astonishingly long tongue. It was at least the length of his arm. This gave Jake the clue he needed and he exclaimed 'Anteater. Of course!' out loud.

At once, the children froze and stared at him as though they had just noticed him. 'Arteetar?' the little boy who had been playing with the tongue said tentatively. Jake guessed that he thought this was his name and said 'No, Jake,' pointing at himself.

Soon all the children caught on and were merrily calling him 'Shake, Shake' and encouraging him to go back to the river with them. This he was very glad to do and soon he was playing happily in the water with them, but he could not get them to tell him their names. He also failed completely to persuade them to play ball with him when he found a suitably shaped lump of wood. They just didn't seem to find catching and throwing interesting, which disappointed him as he was rather good at it. Instead they chased each other a lot and then would suddenly stop and peer carefully into one of the pools when they caught sight of a fish. Then everyone would carefully stalk it, picking up whatever sticks lay about and spearing them into the water. They would also stop whatever they were doing if a lizard or frog appeared and chase that. They seemed much more interested in hunting then in playing games.

When they all raced back to the house as the sun began to set, the old man tutted crossly at the sight of Jake's leaf bandage, which was wet and hanging off in tatters. He made him sit down at once in his hammock and wait while he went to get some fresh leaves and some other dried herbs. These he rubbed into the wound while chanting incantations and Jake realized that he was a real witch doctor.

'Gosh,' he thought. 'I'll be able to tease old Dr Wilkinson if I ever get home with how much better my Indian doctor friend is.'

The wound seemed to be healing well. It was clean and not at all sore any more. The old man did not smile or comfort him at all but Jake felt that he understood him very well, as though he could look inside him. He said 'Can I go home now?' but the old man just took hold of his head and laid him gently back in the hammock.

That night Jake woke up to see and hear the old man performing some sort of ceremony. As he lay in his hammock and watched he could not understand what was going on, but it involved a lot of smoke being blown around and dancing. There was an obviously sick little girl who the Indian would pick up and rock to and fro from time to time, blowing smoke over her. Much later, he woke again to find that he was now being chanted over. The old man was looking deep into his eyes and there seemed to be a message there, but it was hard to stay awake with the smoke and the singing. He felt himself dropping off but instead of sinking into sleep he seemed to go straight into a dream. Only this was no ordinary dream. Unlike the other nights when he had dreamt of home and known it was a dream, this time he was really there. His mother was smiling and holding out her hands to him. His bed, with clean white sheets was ready and waiting. All he had to do was climb into it and go to sleep. His old teddy was on the pillow and, as he sank into a deep, dreamless slumber, he felt completely safe and unafraid for the first time since he had been kidnapped.

13
Hunting

In the morning, he went and squatted beside the old man as he dipped in the pot. He wanted to ask him if he had really sent him home in his dream or if it had all been in his imagination. After all, how could an Indian possibly know about the sort of world he came from? And yet, he felt sure that there was more to it than sheer chance.

Trying to catch his eye, he said 'Home?' to the old man, who ignored him completely, although a faint smile seemed to be twitching at his lips. 'Home?' he asked again, desperation sounding in his voice. Now the lined old face was turned towards him and the deepset eyes looked into his for a moment. It felt as though an electric shock ran through Jake's body and he was never sure afterwards if he had really remained awake or had momentarily fallen asleep, but it seemed to him that the Indian had his teddy bear in his arms and was rocking it gently. A moment later the old man had risen to his feet and was walking towards the entrance. Jake ran after him and stood defiantly in front, barring his way. He had to know what it all meant. With a firm hand he was pushed to the side, but as the Indian walked out of the house he heard the single word 'Home' come from him quite distinctly, followed by a long chuckle.

Feeling strong and ready for anything, Jake returned to the hearth and finished his meaty breakfast. He noticed now that the young man who had brought the anteater back the evening before was there as well and realized that anteater was probably what they were eating. Everything in the pot seemed to taste much the same, though this morning's menu had been a bit richer now he came to think of it.

He looked across at the young man and was pleased to see him smiling at him. Encouraged by this, he made a gesture of drawing a bow. Immediately, the young man got up and fetched two bows and a bundle of arrows from the rafters. Gesturing to Jake to follow him, he walked outside into the sunlight. Handing one of the bows to Jake, he drew the other and sent an arrow whizzing towards a burnt tree stump at the edge of the clearing. It struck the foot and remained sticking up out of the earth. Then he indicated that Jake should have a go.

He thanked his lucky stars that he and Keith had spent so much time practising with his bow at home. This one felt reasonably like his own, although the cord was distinctly harder to draw. He made a few trial pulls, chose an arrow which seemed good and straight and aimed for the top of the trunk. To his relief, the arrow struck true and stayed quivering halfway up. It had been a test and he had passed.

Without any further preparation, they set off together into the forest. Halfway across the clearing

Jake stopped and, pointing at himself, said 'Jake', then pointed at the young Indian. He did not know that Indians are very reluctant to give their real names, which are not used in the same familiar way by them as in our society. Instead, those who have had any contact with non-Indians usually adopt a Christian name to avoid embarrassment. Now his companion muttered 'Pedro' quietly, then broke into a trot and vanished into the forest.

On leaving the sunlight, he could not see Pedro at first and stopped to get his bearings. Then he caught a glimpse of a figure flitting between the trees and at once he was off in pursuit. Pedro ran at a steady trot and Jake had to concentrate not to trip over the many roots which lay across the faint path. This meant that his eyes were on his feet most of the time. But not Pedro's. He seemed to glide across the ground barely touching it and Jake envied the way he made so little noise, his bare feet padding softly on the earth. His own trainers thumped loudly and he tried to do as Pedro did and put his whole foot flat on the ground at each step instead of hitting it heel first. He was just getting the hang of this and feeling rather pleased with himself at how little noise he was making, when Pedro stopped dead and he crashed into him from behind. Pedro was crouched motionless looking up into the canopy and holding his bow at the ready.

Following his gaze, Jake could see something moving slowly above them. At first he thought it was a snake; then he realized that it was the long neck of a large bird which was peering down at them. Barely seeming to move, Pedro was preparing an arrow and cautiously notching it into the string of his bow. Jake was trying to hold his breath and keep his balance on one foot at the same time as seeing what was going on. Something had to give and, sure enough, just as the point of the arrow started to come up, Jake's other foot hit the ground, the bird squawked and flew off, and Pedro turned round to give Jake a look of disgust.

Trotting along behind, he was determined not to let that happen again. He stayed a bit further back, practised running quietly by watching Pedro and noticed how he was constantly spotting things which anyone else would have missed. Barely breaking stride, Pedro would pause for an instant to glance at each living thing they passed. By following each glance, Jake began to realize how much was going on in the forest which he had not noticed during all his long and lonely walking.

Lizards lay along branches and up the trunks of trees, so well camouflaged that only a faint outline betrayed their presence. Higher up, there were squirrels and high in the canopy small monkeys and lots of birds. However insignificant or far away, Pedro would always freeze for a moment to inspect each living thing. Usually he rejected them as being, Jake supposed, too small or too far away to be worth considering as food, but it was fascinating to have so much life revealed. With Pedro he did not feel afraid but began to see the forest as a vast supermarket with shelves full of good things for the taking. And it was not just animals which attracted Pedro's attention. Several times he stopped to gather fungi growing on the ground or on trees. To carry them, he made an instant basket by weaving leaves together and hanging it over his back with a vine cord. Once they came across a bush covered in yellow berries. They reminded Jake of raspberries but were shaped like big blackcurrants and they gorged themselves for a time before gathering some of those as well.

Another bush was covered in caterpillars and these Pedro examined carefully before popping one into his mouth and munching it. Jake declined to join him, but later that evening he saw some of the same caterpillars being roasted on the fire and tried one. It tasted just like fried shrimp.

They stopped to rest on a bridge made by a tree which had fallen across a small stream. In the clear water below some fish were lying, revealed only by their gently waving tails. Very slowly Pedro lowered the point of one of his long arrows into the water. It had a white sliver of bone as the arrow head and barb; they could see this approaching the fish below the surface. Suddenly Pedro struck and, with a scooping motion, brought up a struggling fish impaled on the end. 'I know I couldn't have done that,' thought Jake, but he planned to try it out on the carp in the school pond if he ever got home.

Soon after they had started jogging along again, Pedro slowed the pace to a walk and indicated that they should be very quiet. They came to the edge of an open glade, where the sunlight shone. Peering very cautiously round a tree at the edge, Pedro pointed with an arrow. It took Jake some time to spot what he was pointing at; then he saw that it was a pale brown deer grazing calmly far out in the sunlight. Pedro made it quite clear that Jake should stay where he was and started crawling through the dry undergrowth towards the deer. Every now and then it would throw up its head and look keenly round. As Jake watched he found himself torn between hoping that Pedro would be successful so that they could return in triumph with such a fine prey, and wanting the beautiful creature to escape. Although he had long vanished from Jake's sight and no telltale movement of the bushes showed how far he had crawled, Pedro must have made a false move for the deer suddenly leapt round to look at something, cocked its head on one side as though listening and then bounded off, leaping high into the air each time. Soon it was out of sight and a crestfallen Pedro had returned.

Back in deep forest it was some time before they stopped again and Jake was beginning to feel tired. Now, however, Pedro became very excited and, after listening for a moment, put his hands to his mouth and made a strange hooting sound. It was answered immediately and together this time they crawled forward. Parting some bushes, they looked into a wide area of bare earth where two large black birds like turkeys appeared to be dancing. First one and then the other would strut about, occasionally delivering one of the hoots Pedro had imitated. It must be a mating dance of some sort, thought Jake, but that was not going to deter them. He nudged Pedro and pointed to the left hand bird. Nodding, Pedro began to aim at the right hand one. Together they let fly.

Pedro's bird dropped dead but Jake's ran off squawking, the arrow trailing behind it. Immediately both of them were up and running, whooping as they leapt over bushes in their pursuit. The bird was hard hit and it was not long before they caught up and began to bear down on either side. 'Now I'll show the Indians how we play rugger at home,' thought Jake as he made a flying tackle and grabbed hold of the bird's wings. As they wrestled, it turned to peck at him but before it could do so Pedro had grabbed it as well and wrung its neck.

They lay side by side gasping for breath and laughing. Pedro reached over and patted Jake on the back, saying something in his own language. It could only have been 'Well done!'

Their return to the communal house was the triumph Jake had hoped for and, as he listened to Pedro telling his people about the chase after the turkey, he felt wonderfully safe and almost at home with these kind, hospitable people. Almost. There was a nagging feeling at the back of his mind all the time that he ought to be trying to get a message out or to get out himself somehow. But he was enjoying himself so much and having such an interesting time with the Indians that he couldn't work up much urgency about it. He was also very, very tired and the next day he slept until the afternoon.

14
The Camp

That night the Indians had a party for Jake. At least that was what he decided it was because he seemed to be the centre of attention and everyone was very nice to him. There was a large bowl with a special juice in it which the women had been preparing all day, and there were more people around than there had been previously. He assumed they must have come over for the evening from a neighbouring group. Everyone was in very good spirits and the party began while it was still daylight.

The old man appeared from the other hut wearing a strange straw cape and mask. Even though his head was completely covered, Jake knew it was him. There was something very special about the old man, thought Jake. You could never mistake him for anyone else. Now he settled himself in the middle of the open space and began to chant and beat on a hollow wooden tube. The other men, their bodies colourfully decorated with paint and with scarlet and blue feathers tied to their arms, came out and danced around him. They were carrying their bows and arrows and they waved them high in the air.

The women danced more demurely, in a line. At

the same time they sang a rhythmic chant, while placing one foot at a time in and out. Two of them grabbed Jake and made him dance as well, although he fought hard not to. They just held him between them in the line and he had to do what they did. After a while he began to enjoy it, and anyway it was impossible to be in a bad mood when everyone was having so much fun.

Much later, long after it was dark, he sat with the men and tried to understand the discussion which was taking place. He was pretty sure it was about him and tried out his few words of Spanish to see if he could take part. 'Inglés' produced no reaction, but 'Sendero Luminoso' caused everyone to stop talking and look at him. He tried to mime what had happened to him, pointing an imaginary gun at himself and then pretending to run away. He was pretty sure they got the message. More importantly, the way they reacted to the name of the guerrilla group convinced him that they would not hand him over to them.

He tried 'Pucallpa' but they shook their heads, whether because they did not understand or because they did not want to go there, he was unsure. 'Ucayali', the name of the big river, received a better response and one or two pointed with their chins in the same direction that their own river ran.

'Papá,' he said, remembering that was what Jaime had called his father. They understood that all right and looked sympathetic. He felt sleepy during the long discussion that continued far into the night beside the fire. But he kept hearing the words 'Papá' and 'Padre', which he knew meant father, repeated and it was reassuring to know that so many other people were wrestling with his problem.

In the morning there was a lot of activity. The occupants of the house seemed to be packing up their things as though they were about to depart. Jake thought he had better do the same and it was as well he did because, just as he had everything neatly wrapped, he saw his friend Pedro beckon to him and walk out of the house. Picking up his bundle and the bow and arrows he had been lent the previous day, Jake followed to see Pedro disappearing into the forest. They left just like that; no 'Goodbyes' or 'Thank yous', no backward looks. It was the Indian way, but Jake did not know that and wanted to go back and say goodbye properly, as he had been brought up to do. Especially, he wanted to see the old man again, but he dare not lose sight of Pedro and soon they were too far away for him to be able to find his way back.

After a while, they came to a small clearing with fallen tree trunks in it. Here Pedro dropped his vine hammock and indicated that Jake should leave his bundle as well. They went hunting but, perhaps because Jake was in a bad mood and so made too much noise, they saw nothing and returned empty handed.

To his amazement, they re-entered the clearing to find it full of people. It looked as though everyone from the big house was there and, from the baskets and bundles they were carrying it seemed that they were going to travel with him. Jake was so pleased and relieved to see the old man standing among them that he ran up to him and hugged him. Everyone laughed and looked a bit embarrassed at this unmanly behaviour, but the old man patted him softly on the head and went off to sit by himself on a log.

They walked all day. Everyone carried something, even the children, who had baskets hanging over their backs with a thong round the forehead to take the weight. Only the very smallest children were carried. There were much more frequent stops than there had been when he went hunting and Jake found the going easy. At stops, everyone chattered and larked about. There was an atmosphere of being on a picnic. People would go off into the bushes and come back with a basket of berries or fruit they had collected and these would be shared out at once and eaten on the spot. If anyone had a minor accident, like being stung by a bee or sitting on a thorn, everyone shrieked with laughter. No one ever received any sympathy and yet Jake noticed that the children were always taken great care of, and he never heard one cry.

They were passing one of the forest giants which sometimes soar up above the rest of the forest canopy, when the old man stopped Jake and pointed to one of the highest limbs, perhaps fifty metres up, indicating that he should look at it closely. He could just make out some flying insects hovering around a hole marked by black stains. After a bit of mime, he understood that it was a bees' nest and that there would be honey inside. He shrugged his shoulders to indicate 'So what?', since the tree was clearly unclimbable. The massive trunk rose straight up ten metres before branching and it was smooth with no handholds.

The whole group had now stopped and gathered

round, looking up and pointing at the bees. Jake assumed that it would be one of the young men who would try to climb the tree, but instead it was the old man who dropped his bundle and prepared himself. They had one axe with them, which he strapped to his back; then he went and cut a carefully measured length of liana, one of the creeping vines which hung from many of the trees throughout the forest. This he wrapped around his body. Walking away from the tree he leapt nimbly into the lower branches of a neighbouring tree and disappeared into the foliage. Re-appearing higher up, he was able to reach one of the big tree's extended branches and cross over to the main stem.

By now he was all of thirty metres up but there was still one wide gap above him with no handholds in between. He now unwound and lowered the length of liana to the end of which Pedro attached a long pole which he had been preparing. When he had pulled this up, the old man balanced it at a steep angle between the branch he was standing on and the next one up. He then climbed up it, hand over hand. Now he was able to reach the bees' nest branch easily, but Jake was almost afraid to look, he was now so high up. The old man walked out along the branch almost to the spot where the bees emerged, untied the axe and began to chop the wood beneath his feet. It took some time but at last there was a creaking followed by a crash as the whole branch fell to the ground, leaving a solitary figure high in the sky looking as though he were about to walk the plank.

Everyone hurried over to look and someone produced a smoking brand to flush out the bees and keep them away. Within moments, the old man was there too (Jake thought he must have flown down; by now nothing would have surprised him, but he had not been looking) and he cut the branch open. Inside was a beautiful honeycomb, as well as the white larvae of young bees. These were picked out and passed round to be eaten first. They were sweet and succulent, just like the honey itself. Most of that was wrapped in leaves for later but everyone had a good mouthful. Jake, whose last sweet had been eaten long before his rescue by the Indians, was especially glad to taste something sugary for a change.

In the middle of the afternoon they all stopped. To Jake it looked just like anywhere else in the forest, but the Indians all seemed to know that it was where they would camp. In an astonishingly short space of time they had created a mini village. They cut poles, stuck them upright firmly in the ground and lashed them together with strips of vine. The men carried great piles of palm fronds, invisible under their loads; the women rapidly wove them together to form waterproof roofs. They formed rough platforms for keeping the baskets off the ground, away from ants; they slung hammocks between the poles, lit fires, slung pots over them and soon the smell of smoke and cooking filled the air.

There were some tall palm trees at the place where they had stopped. One of the women pointed out to Jake that there were big bunches of orange and red fruit growing near the tops of some of them and indicated that they were good to eat. Strolling over with the intention of nipping up the tree and throwing some down, he found that the trunk had long, black spikes all the way up. Trying to see if he could climb he soon found that they were sharp when he pricked himself. He was sucking his hand, thinking, when he realized that Pedro was standing beside him and laughing at him. 'Well, you climb it if you're so clever!' he said, crossly. His meaning was clear, even though he spoke in English and Pedro laughed again. Instead of trying to climb the tree itself, Pedro went to the next big one, from which lots of lianas were hanging down. He swarmed easily up these, hand over hand until he was at about the level of the fruit. He then cut off one of the thinner lianas with the machete, which he carried tied to a thong around his waist, and lassoed the fruit tree by throwing a loop over a branch. Now he was able to pull the two trees together until he was able to reach across the narrow gap and cut off a bunch of fruit. They fell to the ground with a crash and scattered. Children ran to gather them up and carry them to their mothers who pounded them in a pot, added water and began to cook them. 'Stewed plums,' thought Jake, as he tucked in, 'that's what they taste like.'

Jake had been interested in seeing how they lit the fires, hoping that they might rub two sticks together. He was disappointed to see a box of matches produced from inside one of the baskets, where it was wrapped carefully in a bunch of dry leaves. He supposed that they must have traded at some time with the outside world, but he noticed that only one match was used and that all the other fires were lit from the first one. He went and sat next to the old man and, indicating the fire, pretended to rub sticks together to light it, then looked up enquiringly. The old man looked at him, thought for a moment and then got up and went to his basket. From it he removed two pieces of wood, one flat, like a tiny plank, with a small scorched hole in the middle, the other a pointed stick. Putting the sharp end of the stick into the hole he began to twirl it very fast between the palms of his hands, backwards and forwards. Jake counted fifty double twirls before a thin curl of smoke appeared in the hole. Pausing for a second, the old man dropped a pinch of dry shavings into the hole and went on twirling, now blowing very gently at the same time. The smoke increased and suddenly there was a flame. He stopped and let it all go out.

The children, who had gathered round when he started, all went 'Whee!' and chattered excitedly among themselves. 'They must have had matches for some time,' thought Jake. Then he thought 'Now I'll show them how I do it' and he took out his Swiss Army knife. Opening the magnifying glass and borrowing the old man's dry shavings, he focused the evening sunshine on to them. Everyone pushed in to see what he was doing and he had to make them stand back so that they did not come between him and the sun. For a time he was afraid that he had left it too late and the sun was no longer strong enough to do the trick, then the telltale wisp of smoke appeared and, soon after, he was able to coax a flame from it. Now the children let out an even louder shriek and everyone wanted to look at and handle his magic knife. The old man came over and, in his unsmiling way, looked at the little fire, looked at Jake and then patted him on the shoulder. He felt prouder than at any time he could remember, better even than when he had scored the winning try in a school rugby match.

Pedro, who had pretended not to be interested, signalled to ask if he wanted to go hunting again. Retrieving his knife and bow he trotted off into the undergrowth. It was quite thick and they had to push through but soon came out on the river bank. Jake had not realized that they were so close, having not seen any trace of it all day. It was wider now and a beach, almost like the seaside, stretched ahead of them. The sun was just setting and it was marvellous to come out into the open after being hemmed in by trees all day. The clouds across the river were piled up high into the sky and the sunlight had turned them pink and orange in a dazzling display.

The strange booming which had frightened him the second night he was alone was echoing across from the far side again and he pointed in that direction to ask Pedro what it was. Quite clearly he mimicked a monkey and when Jake looked doubtful, thinking he must not have understood, he pulled his chin down, opened his mouth and imitated the sound. 'Must be a big monkey!' thought Jake.

They ran across the warm sand, left their bows and, in Jake's case, trousers and shirt on the bank and plunged in for a cooling swim after the long day's walk. As darkness fell they walked on to a lagoon, where an old bend of the river had been cut off to form a lake. It was a marshy area with high rushes, through which they pushed their way slowly and cautiously. Once they could see open water in front of them again, they settled on a bank of higher ground and waited for their eyes to become accustomed to the gloom.

The sounds around them were almost deafening, the evening cicadas vying with the multitude of frogs in the marsh to produce a frightful mixture of sounds which Jake found confusing. Pedro, however, had his eyes fixed on a spot out in the lagoon and clearly had his mind firmly on hunting. He put his hands to his mouth and began to make very strange sounds, halfway between a cough and a grunt. For a while nothing happened and then, following Pedro's gaze, Jake was just able to see a shape moving through the water towards them. With a start he realized that it must be a crocodile and that Pedro had been calling it.

Jake had seen too many Tarzan films not to believe that the crocodile was coming to attack them and he stepped back quickly. Pedro, however, knew that the South American crocodilians, called caimans, very rarely attack people and are by and large rather dozy, harmless creatures. He waited until the animal's head came to rest just below him. Most of it was still submerged, but the end of its snout and its two protruding eyes were visible. Very slowly drawing back his bow, to which he had fitted an arrow with a sharp serrated blade, Pedro fired at point blank range just below the surface and between the eyes. Immediately the caiman started to thrash about. With some rather cautious help from Jake, who still believed that it was going to eat him, Pedro dragged it ashore by the tail and killed it by thrusting the arrow right in.

Although it had looked huge and frightening in the water, it turned out to be less than a metre long. Borrowing Jake's knife, which was sharper and easier to handle than his machete, Pedro removed the tail and carried it back to the camp. Slices were then grilled over one of the fires and everyone gathered around for a piece. Jake was not sure he liked the idea of eating crocodile much, but when he was urged to try some, he found that it tasted just like fish fingers without the breadcrumbs. With his eyes shut, he could even pretend that the ash, with which each piece became coated, *was* breadcrumbs.

The atmosphere in the camp was like a jolly summer's outing. It was nothing like the frightening jungle which had so daunted him when he first found himself alone in it. Everyone was laughing and playing; there was much more noise than in the big house and there was no doubt that all the Indians were enjoying themselves. Then the first big drops of rain fell and he was very glad that they had built such effective shelters. His hammock and Pedro's were close together in one of them and, although the rain suddenly began to come down in a solid sheet, so that it was impossible to see across the clearing, they were completely dry. He didn't even need to hang up his ground sheet in the way it had been used in the guerrillas' hut to stop the drips, as there were no drips.

There was also a good fire in their shelter, which kept them warm during the rain storm and gave plenty of light. Pedro had gone off into the marsh, after killing the caiman, to collect something, and Jake was interested in finding out what it was. All he knew was that Pedro had come back with one of his little instant leaf baskets and that there seemed to be something alive inside. Now Pedro put the basket on the ground between their hammocks and began to unwrap it. To Jake's surprise there were two very pretty little frogs inside. They had bright yellow and green stripes and brilliant orange spots. Instinctively, he put on his hand to touch them. He had always liked frogs.

He was shocked by how hard Pedro hit him. Before his hand was halfway to the frogs his shoulder was struck a mighty blow and he fell back into his hammock. Pedro was tutting furiously and speaking fast in his own language. Then he slowed down and tried some words of Spanish. '*Muy peligrosa! Muy venenosa!*' which Jake understood to mean 'Much danger! Very poisonous!' He watched as Pedro very carefully took some of the spare arrow heads, which he kept in a bamboo quiver over his shoulder, and wiped the tips in the slime on the frogs' backs before holding them out over the fire to dry. If the frogs were so poisonous then he must be using them to make poisoned arrows, thought Jake. He was right. Arrow poison frogs are said to produce the most powerful poison known to man and many of the Indian people discovered this long ago and put it to good use in helping to catch their food.

Rubbing his shoulder, but feeling very safe and at home surrounded by so many friends, Jake fell asleep.

15
The Village

There was a subdued atmosphere next morning as the camp was packed up and at first Jake could not make out what was wrong. No one would look at him and he wondered if he had done something to offend them. Before he realized what was happening, all the Indians started to drift away, but not forwards, downstream. They were returning to their home. He knew he would probably never see any of them again and wanted to run after them, but he had learnt by now that that was not the Indian way. As he gazed sadly after the disappearing figures, none of whom looked back at him, the girl who had brought him the soup when he first woke up in their house, ran back and forced a bracelet over his wrist. He looked down and saw that it was made of colourful wild red seeds, woven together with a strip of fine black wood. Before she ran back to join the rest he glimpsed her face and saw that there were tears streaming down it. Now that he had noticed, he realized that many of the others were quietly crying too.

Soon only Pedro and the old man were left. Without a word, the three of them set off downstream.

They walked fast and in silence, each lost in his

own thoughts. Even Pedro seemed uninterested in hunting for once. The character of the forest changed after a while and the Indians became alert and watchful again. There were man-made clearings, which they skirted and once they crossed a deeply rutted track made by vehicles. They must be nearing 'civilization', and Jake's heart leapt at the thought that he might soon be reunited with his father. The Indians, on the other hand, became more and more nervous.

At last they came to the edge of the forest and stopped. They were on a low hill, looking down on a village with the wide Ucayali river flowing past the end of the main street. It was a scruffy little place only consisting of a few dozen houses and there didn't seem to be anyone about. Jake could feel that the Indians were afraid of the place and did not want to go any further. This was his world that he was on the edge of now and he must go on alone. Feeling very sad, he turned to the old man and bowed his head, trying to think all the thanks he wanted to say for saving him, mending his arm — and for much more. He knew that the old man could see inside his mind and that language was not necessary between them. Expressionlessly, he reached out his skinny old hands and held Jake's temples between them. Jake felt a wonderful lightness, as though he would never have a headache again, and closed his eyes. When he re-opened them the old Indian was sitting on the ground some distance away with his back to him.

Pedro was looking worried. He was staring at the village and something seemed to be bothering him. When Jake tried to say goodbye he shook his head

112

and pointed at the church which stood near the river. Smoke was coming from it. Although he would clearly have preferred to return to his forest home, Pedro had made up his mind that he must accompany Jake until he was sure he was safe and so they started walking across the open ground together. As they left the shelter of the last tree, Jake heard quite distinctly the single word 'Home' waft out of the forest to him followed by a soft chuckle.

The village seemed to be abandoned and they kept to the small patches of afternoon shadow as they skirted the poor houses. Some of the doors were open and the contents had been ransacked. A dog snarled at them but ran off whimpering when they turned towards it. Near the church they stopped. It seemed impossible to Jake that there could be nobody about and he thought of shouting to see if anyone came. But one look at Pedro's face dissuaded him. He was not just a frightened Indian unused to being in a town. He knew something and Jake was not at all sure that he wanted to share the knowledge.

There was smoke coming from the church and that was not right. No one lit fires in a church and anyway the smoke was coming from one of the broken windows. Very cautiously they crept past a bar on the last corner of the street. Glancing inside, Jake could see that the stools were all unoccupied although there appeared to be someone lying behind the bar counter. 'Drunk, I suppose,' he muttered, looking at the man's bare feet.

The door of the church was open and the modest porch was in deep shadow. They felt safer once they reached that and paused before looking inside. It felt to Jake as though the village was holding its breath.

As soon as they stepped into the nave of the church, they smelt the smell and heard the buzz of flies. There were bodies everywhere, sprawled in the aisle and across the pews. Blood lay in drying pools on the hard earth floor and there were bullet marks pitting the plaster walls. These were not people who had crawled into the church to die. They had been massacred there. At the altar lay the body of the priest. His arms outstretched, he lay face downwards. A candle had fallen and set fire to the altar cloth and it was this that had produced the smoke they had seen from the hill. Pointing at the priest's body, Pedro said 'Padre' and Jake understood that this had been the man they were taking him to, not his father.

Looking at the terrible scene of death, Jake felt the same awful slow motion stillness coming over him that he had felt when he saw Manolo shot. He couldn't move but stood rooted to the spot, his mouth open, his eyes wide. Then Pedro grabbed him by the arm and turned him round; and then they ran.

Blindly they ran towards the river. Jake had to stop on the way to be sick. He had never seen a dead body before, except Manolo's, and he had been face down in the water. Now he just wanted to get away from that place. Perhaps there would be a boat they could take.

On the waterfront, which was really just a steep earth bank, there were indeed a few boats. In particular there was one covered launch with *Buena Vista* painted in large letters at the bow and stern which seemed to have people on it. There was movement and it was rocking slightly on the water. Jake hesitated and suddenly there was the sound of gunfire, not far away just on the other side of the village. He looked in an agony of indecision at Pedro. The Indian pointed firmly at the boat, tapped him once on the shoulder just where he had hit him the night before and left, running through the shadows.

Jake ran to the boat. A voice hissed at him, he stumbled on deck and hands helped him down out of sight. He saw a huddle of women and children and a very fat man from whom sweat was pouring as though he were a sponge. 'He's frightened,' thought Jake, 'and so am I!'

The fat man was fussing about, trying to untie ropes and picking up a pole to push ineffectually at the bank, which did no good as the boat was still tied up. Jake could see that he was in a state of complete panic. After what he had just seen in the church, Jake could hardly blame him but, to his surprise, he felt completely calm. Taking out his knife and opening the big blade, which had the fat man cowering in a corner gibbering with fear, he quickly cut the ropes and then easily pushed the boat out into the stream. Luckily, it ran fast at that point and soon the craft was gathering speed and leaving the village behind. Looking back, Jake could see puffs of smoke coming from some men who had rushed out on to the waterfront. It was not until he heard the bangs that he realized they were shooting at him, but by then they were out of range.

As the last house on the outskirts of the village drifted past, he stood up to stare hard at the fringe of forest looming over the top of the small hill. For a moment he glimpsed two figures as they stepped out into the sunshine and held their arms out to him before vanishing back into the shadows.

16
The River

Inside the boat were three women and five small children as well as the fat man. They were all in a state of hysteria, screaming if Jake touched or even came near them. They lay huddled together in a triangular space under the bows. Waving goodbye to his Indian friends had, in some strange way, made Jake feel even calmer and more in control of himself. It was almost as if the old man had sent a message of strength and self-confidence across the space between them as a last present to Jake, to speed him on his way. Now he found that, as the only person on board who was not hysterical, it seemed perfectly natural to him to take charge. He tried, unsuccessfully, to talk to the children, to calm them down, to stop them screaming but having no success went back on deck. The fat man followed him, watching him suspiciously from piggy little eyes which were almost buried behind folds of flesh. He did not seem ready to make friends, in spite of the fact that he would probably have been dead by then if Jake had not miraculously appeared.

The boat was now well out in the stream and drifting fast. However, they weren't going to get anywhere in a hurry like that and Jake went down below again to see if there was an engine. There was! What was even better was that Jake recognized it, or at least he knew exactly what sort it was. On the farm they had a diesel generator which was used to power his stepfather Philip's carpentry workshop. Jake had been taught how to start this and had often done so. This boat engine looked just like the one at home. It even had the same brass starting handle at one end. Checking that the levers were in the right position, he swung the handle and, to his astonishment, the engine started at once.

The fat man now came puffing down, muttering and fiddling officiously with all the levers Jake had already set. Ignoring him, Jake went up to the wheel house, pushed the big lever there forward and, as he felt the engine engage and begin to push the boat along, took hold of the wheel and started to steer. Guessing that Pucallpa must be back upstream, he put the wheel over and began to turn into the current. Feeling the boat change direction, the fat man scrambled back up on deck and started to scream shrilly at Jake. When he stopped for a moment, Jake said 'Pucallpa?' enquiringly pointing ahead. At this the fat man became even more agitated. Jake gathered that Pucallpa did indeed lie back upstream but that the fat man did not want to go there. Jake wondered why. The river was wide and they should easily be able to get past the village without being seen or shot at. But when he tried to explain this in his poor Spanish, the fat man suddenly pulled a gun out of his jacket pocket and pointed it at Jake.

Feeling unreal after all the excitements and horrors of the last few hours, Jake did as he was bid and turned the boat back downstream. Did the fat man think he was one of the guerrillas? Presumably it was the *Sendero Luminoso* who had committed the atrocity in the village. If so, then he didn't much mind continuing to head away from them, even if his father might still be in Pucallpa. Whatever the fat man's reasons, he was content to go along with them, for the time being at least. They would reach somewhere eventually and then he would be able to get a message to his father somehow. The fat man put his gun away.

The *Buena Vista* was a well-equipped boat, Jake found, when the fat man took the wheel and he went to explore. There were several drums of diesel oil, so they could go as far as they liked if the engine didn't break down. There was also lots of food and some sacks full of white stuff stacked under a tarpaulin. Jake was hungry but did not feel that he could just help himself and the fat man was so unpredictable that he was afraid to ask him. It was a relief, therefore, when one of the women eventually stirred herself, stopped crying and began to cook a meal.

During the next few days, life improved for all on board. As they chugged on down the wide river they all began to behave more normally. The other women recovered from their shock and began to help. The children must have seen things that were even more horrible than those Jake and Pedro had stumbled on, and they remained silent and withdrawn. The fat man continued to behave very strangely and Jake did his best to keep out of his way. But he let Jake steer the boat and Jake enjoyed that a lot. It was a good feeling with the deck beneath his feet and the wide river stretching out ahead. They passed a few villages visible in the distance on one or other of the banks, but when Jake suggested stopping the gun was brought out again. They caught some fish by trailing a hook with meat on it over the side and at night they tied up by an island or at a remote stretch of bank. Jake slung his hammock at the stern away from the others, who seemed frightened of him. He had brought the bow and arrows Pedro had lent him on board, not having had time to give them back as they parted. He felt bad about that as he had not intended keeping them, but he knew that Pedro could make more and that it would not be a serious loss. One evening he left the boat and walked along the bank to a lagoon where he was able to shoot a duck sitting on the water. 'Not very sporting,' he thought, 'but I don't think I could hit one flying.'

Even when he brought the duck back and helped pluck it for supper, the women were no more friendly to him. He saw them whispering to each other and pointing at his bow. He could not understand why they should be frightened of him. They seemed unable to accept him and he supposed that to them he was a mysterious creature who had appeared out of nowhere at a nightmare moment. Not speaking their language probably made him stranger and he guessed that he must seem almost Indian to them. His clothes were ragged and dirty and they had heard him use the forbidden words 'Sendero Luminoso'. They made sure that their children kept well away from him.

The river narrowed. Mountains crowded in on

either side and the current began to run faster. The fat man was steering; Jake took the long pole and went to stand in the bows. He had done this sometimes to test the depth of the river when they were passing over shallows and sandbars; now he might have to fend off rocks. Ahead there was a straight line across the surface of the water and Jake could not see what lay beyond. By the time he could see, it was too late to turn back. The river just seemed to fall away into space.

'Stop!' he shouted, and the fat man cut the engine. That was not what Jake had meant. Now they had no control and were at the mercy of the river.

It was not a sheer waterfall like Niagara, more a long, steep slope down which the water flowed evenly. As a result, although the feeling of inevitable doom grew on them as they gathered speed, the sensation itself was quite pleasant and their passage smooth. Then they were travelling much too fast, the walls of rock were hemming them in on either side and something white and noisy lay ahead.

The boat rounded a curve and ran straight into a wall of water. Jake had noticed that there was often a wave at the end of small rapids but this was like an Atlantic breaker about to crash onto a beach. Their boat plunged deep in and the bow disappeared into the wave. Before he could do anything to save himself, Jake was underwater. The force threw him backwards, he struck his head on something and lost consciousness. Luckily, he was not thrown overboard but wedged into the well in front of the wheel house. As he lay there, the bows were pushed by the boat's momentum through the wave and the water fell away on either side leaving them to bob safely among the choppy waves.

When Jake regained consciousness, his first thought was relief that he was alive and still on board. Then he became aware that the fat man was keening like a frightened child. Indeed, when he sat up and looked around he could see that all the women and children were on deck and that they, too, were crying. At first he could not see what they were in such a state about; then he stood up to see better.

They were in the middle of the river, still between high cliffs. The water was flowing very fast but they seemed hardly to be moving. Instead they were rotating gently round in a circle. It was when he looked into the centre of the circle that he saw what it was that had so unnerved the others. The water disappeared down a hole and it looked as though quite soon they would be going that way too. They were in a huge whirlpool, just like the one which forms above a plug hole in a bath when the water is let out, but unimaginably bigger.

It was easy to watch the hole creep nearer each time they circled it and to wait like frightened rabbits for the inevitable to happen. This seemed to be the state into which the others had fallen and for a while Jake, too, found himself incapable of movement. A wave slapped against the side of the boat and the water splashed onto Jake's face. Suddenly realizing that he was soaked to the skin, he tore his eyes away from the gaping hole, shook himself like a dog, pushed the hair out of his eyes and ran below. The engine, to his relief, looked dry and he swung the handle. Nothing happened. He swung it again and again, frantically. Still nothing. He checked the levers. All in the right position. Hurriedly he scrambled back and went into the wheel house. Sure enough, the fat man had switched the engine off and left the switch up. Desperate with haste now, he flicked the switch down and ran back below. As he went, he glanced over the side and saw that they were right on the lip of the hole and for an awful moment he looked into what seemed a bottomless pit. Then he was back at the engine and this time it started with the first swing.

Back in the wheel house there was no time to look again; just to turn the wheel against the current and, as he held his breath, feel the boat respond and gradually begin to climb out of the whirlpool. It seemed to take an age but at last they were back in the choppier waters of the main river and Jake was able to turn the boat's bows to face directly downstream.

There were more rapids and more frightening moments, as they had to fend themselves off passing rocks, but nothing as bad again. With the fat man bossily back at the helm as though he had been there all the time and the boat in calm water again, the banks receded into the distance once more and they continued on their way.

Now the river water became much more cloudy, with silt and mud banks instead of sandy beaches. There was no more forest on the banks, which were cleared of all big trees, and they began to pass great rafts of logs being floated down river. Jake had learnt about the destruction of the rainforests and now he was seeing for himself what it meant.

Yet still the fat man showed no sign of wanting to

stop and so they went on day after day until Jake began to lose all sense of time. He became preoccupied and worried, chafing at the time it was all taking and the feeling that he was getting further away from his father all the time. Although his geography of the region was a bit vague, he remembered his father saying on the flight over the Andes that all the rivers now ran into Brazil, the Amazon and the Atlantic. It had been this idea that he was at least heading towards England and home that had comforted him as he headed away from where he had been kidnapped, but he also realized that he must by now have crossed into Brazil and he was dimly aware that problems might lie that way, too. He also began to feel very ill. For some time he had not wanted to eat the greasy beans and rice which the women prepared but he had thought he was just sick of the taste. Now he noticed that he felt hot and feverish a lot of the time, just like when he had had flu at home, only this came and went so that for some of the time he felt fine. But he still did not want to eat. At last he collapsed and lay alternately sweating and shivering in his hammock. The women still ignored him, though one of them brought him water to drink when he cried out. He felt awful.

It was only when they landed at a village and he heard some men come aboard that he began to take an interest in life again.

17
Smugglers

The men came late at night and they talked in whispers. Jake awoke and, cautiously raising his head, saw that they were moored some distance from a row of street lights but that where they were it was pitch dark. As a result he never saw their faces, but he heard their voices and there was something chilling about the way they spoke. Each word was spat out as though in anger and fear. He could recognize the fat man's ingratiating whisper. The women and children seemed to have gone.

Hoping they would not notice him, he lay still. They were carrying the sacks of white powder up from the hold and they had to pass right past his hammock. The stealth with which they moved, the atmosphere of guilt about their actions made him put two and two together at last and come up with a certain four. The powder must be drugs, the men were drug dealers and he had helped smuggle it all into Brazil.

He was working all this out for the first time; having been feeling too ill to think properly for so long, when one of the men bumped into his hammock, swore loudly, and dropped his sack on the deck with a crash. Immediately all the others gathered round and were prodding at him. One shone a torch in his face. He pretended to be asleep. He could hear the fat man explaining him away in a high whine. He guessed that he wanted to keep him as crew for the return journey. Knowing what an incompetent the fat man was, he could understand why. Meanwhile, he could see through his half-closed eyes that someone was pointing a gun at him. Terrified, Jake lay very still.

The argument raged on, the voices growing louder as the men divided into two camps. It seemed to Jake than one lot were in favour of kill-ing him while the others, of which the fat man was a member, wanted to spare him. He would have liked to take part but thought it better to stay apparently asleep.

Suddenly they all stopped arguing and were silent, listening. A whistle had sounded somewhere on the shore. The torch was put out and the men left him and tiptoed off along the boat. Jake felt sure that something was about to happen. Whatever it was he did not want to be part of it. He could feel fear all around him. Fear and anger and antici-pation. It was like being in a thunderstorm when there is a sudden lull between flashes of lightning. The darkness on board was total and the silence complete. He decided that the moment had come to escape. Quietly, he slipped out of the hammock, felt for the handrail and rolled over the side. Hang-ing by his hands, he could feel his feet in the water and when he let go he dropped into it with barely a splash. It was quite warm and although he did not like the idea of what other creatures might be swim-ming about with him, anything was better than

126

looking down the barrel of that gun. He was at the stern and he could see the reflections of the street lights on the still surface of the river. It was very quiet.

Without warning, he was dazzled by a blinding light. The boat and the whole area around it was suddenly lit up by brilliant spotlights all coming on simultaneously. It was still quiet for a few moments after they turned the floodlights on. Everything on board was as bright as in daylight. Jake could imagine how exposed the men must feel up on deck. With only his head above water, he was almost invisible.

Then the firing began. The first shot came from the deck above his head and one of the floodlights went out. Immediately there was a deafening fusillade from the shore and he could feel the hull of the boat trembling under the impact of hundreds of bullets. There were a few screams, crashes and the tinkle of broken glass before the shooting stopped. Then there were shouted orders and the tramp of feet in heavy boots overhead. Jake stayed very quietly where he was. He wondered if the fat man was still alive. Alive or dead, he was a criminal and that made Jake one too. If he showed himself he would probably be shot and even if he wasn't he could never explain that he was not really a smuggler. They would put him in prison and he would never get home.

He heard bodies being dragged ashore. A vehicle drove up, doors slammed and it drove away. Voices receded in the distance. Everyone seemed to have left. He was just about to swim ashore and climb up the bank when the street lights went out. As he waited for his eyes to re-adjust to the darkness, he caught a glimpse of something red high on the bank. It was too bright to be a glow-worm or a low star and, as he watched it, he saw it move. At once it glowed much brighter and he could see the outline of a face behind it. They had left a guard behind and he was smoking.

His first plan had been to escape into the town and try to find someone he could confide in. Clearly, this was not now possible as he was pretty sure the guard would shoot first and ask questions afterwards if he tried to creep past him. The only thing left for him to do was to get back on board but that wasn't going to be easy either.

The edge of the river was soft mud and he had to move extremely slowly to avoid squelching. The only way, he found, to move silently around the boat to where a plank lay between the deck and the shore, was to lie in the water and 'walk' himself along the shore with his hands. This was not very nice as he kept feeling horrible slimy things and sometimes nasty sharp things like old tin cans. It took him a long time.

Climbing on to the plank and so on board posed the biggest problem. For a start it was the spot nearest to the guard. It was also the most difficult operation to perform silently. He thought of swimming round to the other side of the boat and trying to climb straight up the hull, but he doubted if he would be strong enough and in any case he was beginning to shiver after being wet for so long. Worse, the guard had finished his cigarette and flicked it into the river. It had landed right beside Jake and given him a fright, as he assumed the man would be idly watching where it fell and might see him. He lay still for a while below the plank. Then, blending with the chorus of riverside frogs, which had started up unconcernedly as soon as the shooting stopped, he heard the clear sound of someone snoring.

When it came to the point, it was easier than he had expected to climb on board. The main problem was the sound the water made dripping off his body as he emerged from the river. This, however, was masked by the splashing of the current against the hull. The fact that there was a current at that point was reassuring as it was a necessary part of Jake's plan. Once again, as at the village where he had first boarded the boat, he used his trusty knife to cut through the ropes leading to the bank. One of them fell into the river with a splash and he heard the guard grunt in his sleep. Very gently, he pulled the plank on board and waited for the boat to drift off. It remained where it was, stuck on the mud.

The long pole lay in the bows. Putting one end onto the bank he pushed with all his might. Still no movement. It was only when he had crept to the stern and tried from there that he felt the boat give a little and gradually after that he was able to ease her away from the side.

The current was not very fast and he had to wait for ages before he dared start the engine. Even then it was extremely difficult to see where he was going and he strained his eyes into the darkness, terrified that he would hit a sandbank and be found in the morning in full view. This made him think about how there would almost certainly be a search made for the boat. When the guard saw that the ropes had been cut, he would realize that there must have still been one of the smugglers alive on board and they would come looking for him. He would have to hide.

Through the night he chugged on downstream without hitting anything. As soon as the first light of dawn began to sharpen the outline of river bank, he pulled in closer to it and started to search for a hiding place. The bank at that point was a cliff of sheer yellow soil falling straight into the water. A boat moored against that would be visible for miles. As the sun crept over the horizon he began to feel desperate. They must have noticed that he had gone by now and soon they would come looking. Then he saw it.

To a casual observer it looked as though a tree had fallen in to the river from a low section of the bank. But when he steered closer, he realized that it concealed the narrow entrance to a creek. Carefully manoeuvring the boat into this, he found that it opened up into a lagoon where the vegetation grew up high. There was a perfect spot where he could hide the boat so that even someone looking into the creek from the river would not be able to see it. There were trees all over the bluffs on both sides of the entrance, which lay a short distance in from the main river, but the lagoon itself was big enough to turn the boat round and moor deep in the reeds. Some ducks flew up from the still surface as he did so, a heron took off from a dead tree and various creatures slithered into the water. He could even step ashore from there and so, taking his bow and arrows, he did so. It was easy to make his way back to the bank above the river. There he selected a place among the trees from which he could see up and down the river and waited. He did not have to wait long.

The sound of a high-powered outboard motor reached him long before he could see the speed-boat. When it flashed into view it was an impressive sight. There was a machine gun mounted on the bow, there were four heavily armed soldiers on board and it was travelling very fast. He lay flat on the ground as they approached. One of them fired a burst at the fallen tree, but they were going so fast they failed to notice the creek behind it and, to Jake's huge relief, they sped on.

Now at last he had time to examine the damage to the boat. There were bullet holes everywhere and the glass in the wheel house was broken but otherwise it seemed to be in good shape. One of the sacks of powder had been left in the hold. This he dragged up on deck and tipped over the side. It made the water of the lagoon cloudy and several fish floated to the surface. He checked the fuel drums and found that half of them were still full. Luckily, being below the deck, none had been hit and punctured. There were some tins of sardines, sacks of rice and some of the black beans he had become so fed up with. He could last for weeks on what he had, if need be. What he had to do first was to sit down and make a plan.

First of all, was he a thief to have taken the boat? He supposed he was but he couldn't see what else he could have done without getting shot. Also the fat man was obviously a crook and so it didn't really count to steal from him, did it? He wrestled with

131

his conscience for a time, then decided to give up worrying about that. It was more important to decide which way he should go. Back upstream was where his father might still be, but going there would mean passing both last night's town and the village where the massacre had happened and he didn't want to go to either of those places again, ever. Also he was not sure he would be able to get through the rapids again on his own. He had no idea what lay downstream, except that the river must eventually lead to the Atlantic and his home was on the other side of that. He could think of no better plan.

18
The Amazon

Having made the decision to go on downstream, he spent the rest of the day tidying up the boat. If it was going to be his home, he wanted everything shipshape. Now that the fat man and the slovenly women and children were gone, he became quite house-proud and began to look forward to being captain of his own ship. He had not done much boating before but he had read all the Swallows and Amazons books as well as *Treasure Island* and *Robinson Crusoe* and he had often imagined what it would be like. Now he was going to find out.

During the afternoon, he heard the speedboat coming back and watched it racing up the far distant shore. As it was so late, he decided to stay where he was for that night and set off again the next morning. This gave him a chance to go hunting and see if he could put all Pedro had taught him to good use. So as not to get lost, he stuck to the river bank. There seemed to be less game about than when he had been with the Indians, or perhaps it was just that he was not as good yet at seeing it. He only had four arrows and he was anxious not to loose any of them in useless shots. Instead, he returned to the lagoon, out of which the cloudy water and the dead fish had now drifted, and fished successfully for piranha. There was even a box of matches on board so that he was able to light the stove and cook them properly. His best discovery in the food locker was a large block of solid brown sugar. The women had kept that from him, feeding it to their children. Now he had it to himself and could cut slices off with his knife whenever he felt like it. He had been missing sweet things since the honey the old Indian had gathered.

He slept in his usual place in his hammock. When he first climbed in, he could not make out why it felt different. Some of the cord had broken and his blanket was lumpy. It was only when he shook the blanket out and saw that it was full of holes as though moths had been at it, that he realized how many bullets would have hit him if he had still been there when the shooting started.

There were no disturbances in the night, but he took the precaution of mooring the boat out in the lagoon and away from the shore so that nothing could creep on board. And he was awake before dawn, poling out into the river, starting up the engine and steaming away straight into the sunrise.

Jake now travelled for several days without having a lot of time to think about where he was going or what lay ahead. Navigating the boat, feeding himself, fishing over the side, checking the engine and that everything was shipshape above and below decks; that took up nearly all his time. He found that the routine he made for himself stopped him worrying, although the nagging fear that he would never see his family again was always with him.

The river became so big that he could not see

one bank from the other. Navigation was easy as there was flood water coming down. He did make a few mistakes and touch the bottom but each time the force of the water lifted the boat off again. The biggest hazards he had to watch out for were whole floating trees being swept along on the flood. Some of them were rolling over and over as they moved along, their roots and branches flailing the air before crashing back into the water. If he came too close to one of them it could sink him. Otherwise he saw little activity on the river. There were plenty of other boats, large and small, but it was quite easy to avoid them by crossing to the far side and no one seemed interested in chasing him.

He felt less safe at night and he tried to moor on islands as far as possible. He hardly used the oil lamp, which was difficult to light in any case and usually curled up in his hammock as soon as it was dark. Then it was easy to listen and imagine things. Sound carried long distances on still nights and sometimes he could hear music from passing boats. He longed to go and talk to them but didn't dare as he had no way of knowing whether they would be friendly and no way of explaining that he was not a criminal, as the police would undoubtedly believe if they found the boat. One night some drunken people in a canoe did try to come aboard, but he banged loudly on an empty oil drum he had brought up on to the deck and the noise scared them away. After that he placed on deck the drawing pins, which he had carried with him in his hat band all the way from the guerrillas' camp. Anyone stepping on one of them in bare feet would get a nasty shock, he thought; but mostly it was he who stepped on them in the morning before he remembered to pick them up. Then, in the middle of one night, when he was sleeping soundly, he was awoken by a terrible shout of pain followed by a splash and the sound of a canoe being paddled hurriedly away. That was very satisfactory and he only wished he had someone to share the pleasure with him.

After a while he tried travelling at night. The moon was almost full again by now and so he supposed that it must be about a month since he had been kidnapped. It was quite easy to see the river in the moonlight and it was pleasantly cool, too. The danger came from other boats, as they could not see him. He could see them as they all had some sort of navigation lights but it was difficult to judge how far away they were. Several times he was nearly run down, once by an enormous sea-going vessel which suddenly loomed right over him and scared the daylights out of him by blowing its hooter. He practically scraped along the high black side, which blotted out the light and then he was in the wash and his little craft was being tossed from side to side. All the things he had tidied away below crashed out of their shelves and lockers, water slopped over the sides and he thought he was going to sink. Although this incident gave him a nasty fright, it also encouraged him to believe that he must be approaching civilization again.

Sure enough, the next night he saw a glow in the sky ahead. That could only mean that a big city lay there. He felt excited and frightened at the same time at the prospect of ending his long, lonely journey. He would have to find someone who would understand him and to whom he could explain who he was, but he still had no idea how he was going to do that.

Sunrise revealed houses, lots of them, surrounding a huge river port where ships of all sizes were moored. There were even small skyscrapers along the river front and from far out in the river he could already hear the noise of traffic and car horns. The land rose behind the port and on the hill were grander houses set in their own gardens. Some of them had flags flying and suddenly, with a heart-stopping jolt, he recognized one of them as the Union Jack. That was the house he must try to get to. They would understand. But first he would have to cross through the centre of the town. Taking a deep breath, he pointed the boat at the port and started looking for somewhere to moor.

19
The City

Navigating between so much other shipping when he had been used to being on his own was very confusing. Before he was anywhere near a dock, he had been shouted at several times and he became flustered as he realized that he was drawing attention to himself. This only made things worse and soon he was at the centre of an angry mob of people on boats and on shore shouting advice and abuse at him. Of course, he couldn't understand a word any of them were saying. Then he saw the police.

There were six of them and they were running down the street towards the dock to which he was steering and he was certain that it was him they were after. The Spanish name *Buena Vista* must have stuck out like a sore thumb among all the Brazilian names. Jake guessed that someone in authority had spotted it through his binoculars, checked his records and found that it had been reported stolen. The policemen looked pretty enthusiastic and confident that they were going to get their man.

Jake turned the wheel full over and tried to escape, but it was too late. He was already too far into the harbour to get out in one manoeuvre.

Instead he cut a sideways swathe through all the rest of the shipping sailing or steaming in and out, and the crescendo of abuse rose to deafening proportions. By now he knew enough of the Brazilian character to realize they like a good drama and so was not surprised to find himself the centre of attention. Soon every boat in the harbour was blowing its hooter, cars on the land began to join in and all eyes were fixed on the *Buena Vista*.

After managing by a hair's breadth to avoid hitting anything, the boat was heading up a narrow creek with mud banks on either side and Jake realized that this was it. There was no way out and no room to turn. Ahead was a broken down old dock and beyond that no more water. 'At least there don't seem to be any people,' he thought. There was now a jumble of run-down shacks and narrow alleys between him and the running policemen. 'I just might be able to make a run for it,' he muttered through clenched teeth.

A piercing whistle cut through the harbour's din at that moment and he turned his head to see where it came from. He was passing a ruined wharf which stuck out over the mud into the water. On the end stood a group of ragged children with one larger boy at their head. It was he who had whistled; now he beckoned. There was something about him which made Jake obey instantly. Hauling the wheel over to the left he drove straight at the dock and crashed into it. The boat ploughed into the mud below and came to a sudden stop. He switched off the engine and found himself face to face with one of the strangest people he had ever seen.

The tall boy was black with a mop of dishevelled

white hair and he had a livid scar down one cheek. His clothes were filthy, but he wore them with a swagger and he had a smile to which Jake at once responded. There was a second's stillness and then the boy gestured urgently that Jake should jump ashore. Hurriedly he threw the big brown lump of sugar, which he had kept in the wheel house to nibble at, to the other children, who scrambled for it. Diving below, he grabbed his hat and the bow and arrows. There wasn't time to take down the hammock and so he just took a quick last look and ran.

He ran straight from the boat on to the dock and kept running. He could hear the whistles of policemen now and angry shouts very close. He couldn't see how they could possibly get away, but his new companions seemed to know the area intimately. They ducked under some fallen timbers and were in an open concrete drain. Running up this they came to a round, black hole and were instantly in the dark. One of the children grabbed his hand and he ran on blindly, his feet splashing through shallow water so that his trainers were soaked, until suddenly there was light ahead again. It flooded through a broken crack in the concrete. The tall boy was peering through and motioning the others to keep out of sight. Then, at his signal, they all scrambled through and ran across an open space and into a shabby looking hut.

It was small and it was dirty but it was clearly home for the boys. There were some rags on the floor, a couple of tin mugs and very little else. Except in one corner, where someone had built something like a desk out of bits of packing cases.

There was a box in front for a seat, papers were piled on the desk and there was a mug full of new, coloured biros. It looked extraordinary and out of place in such a poor setting, as though someone were playing at having an office.

He was about to go over and have a closer look when he felt himself jumped on from behind and the next thing he knew he was on the ground with half a dozen very smelly urchins sitting on top of him. He was bigger than any of them but they were strong and they had him well outnumbered. However much he struggled, he could not move. They were going through his pockets, which did not reveal much until they came to his trouser pocket and pulled out the Swiss Army knife. On finding this they all got very excited and it was passed around admiringly. The tall boy, who had taken no part in the fight with Jake, snapped his fingers and the boy holding the knife gave it to him at once. Thoughtfully, he opened the blades one by one, looked through the magnifying glass, pulled out the tweezers and felt the corkscrew. He gestured to the boys to let Jake go and, when he stood up, asked him something in a language he did not understand. It sounded a bit like Spanish but wasn't.

'No comprendo,' said Jake '*Hablo poquito español. Soy inglés.*' He was rather proud to have strung such a long speech together and it seemed that the tall boy had understood that he was speaking in Spanish and that he was English. 'Inglés, eh?' he said and looked again at the knife, caressing it gently with his fingers. Jake could tell that he wanted it very much and was therefore surprised when he

141

sighed and handed it back. The other boys were surprised, too, and set up a great clamour, but the tall boy silenced them with a hiss.

'*Mi nombre es* Jake,' said Jake and the tall boy gave a little formal bow and said '*Eu sou Orlando*' in reply. In spite of his grotesque appearance and ragged clothes, there was a peculiar dignity about the boy, who seemed to Jake to be about his own age, and there was no doubt that the others looked up to him with something close to worship. Now Jake thought that he could walk across the hut to the desk and have a closer look. Orlando was there before him and standing defensively in front of it. '*Por favor,*' said Jake and the other stood aside.

The papers were young children's alphabets, with pictures of animals to represent the letters. There were also simple sums. They were the sort of thing he had grown out of six or seven years before but he could see that they were important to Orlando, who fingered them tenderly. He was, Jake realized, teaching himself to read and count and he wondered if, in the same situation, he would have bothered.

The boys seemed to be a gang of orphans with no homes to go to or families to worry about them. Jake had read that many children live rough on the streets in Brazil and these must be some of them. He had also read that most of them could not expect to live long in the dangerous underworld of a Brazilian city. Wanting to help Orlando, he picked up one of the biros and was about to write something on a big of paper, when it was snatched from his hand and he was pushed away from the desk. It seemed no one was allowed to touch anything on it.

Politely but firmly, Jake took the piece of paper back and placed it on the desk as Orlando stood tensely beside him. He was not used to having his authority questioned. Slowly, in big letters, Jake wrote 'ORLANDO' on the piece of paper.

He could see the tall boy's lips spelling out the letters and beginning to smile. Soon they were hunched side by side writing busily together. Jake was amazed at how quickly the other boy learned. As soon as he wrote something down Orlando copied it quickly and neatly. As soon as he set him a question, either by pointing at a picture or writing down a sum, it was answered. He could feel the urgency to learn in the other and guessed that he had probably never had a teacher before in his life. It gave him a feeling of responsibility and the time passed rapidly. Before they knew it the light was fading and it was evening.

While the two older boys were working the little ones lay on the floor, wrapped themselves in the rags and slept. It looked as though they had not slept all night and Jake wondered how they survived. There was no food in the hut and they had wolfed down the block of sugar straightaway. He wished he had had time to bring more of the supplies from the boat. He had not been planning to lose any time in trying to get to the house with the flag, only now he thought it better to go along with whatever the boys were up to rather than tell them about what he wanted to do. That moment would come.

Orlando now clapped his hands and spoke rapidly to the other boys. As Jake watched in amazement, the ragged group formed into two ranks and stood to attention. Orlando inspected them, lightly cuffing one of them who was chewing something and removing Jake's filthy old handkerchief from the fist of another. Tossing that back to Jake, who shoved it in his pocket, Orlando gave an order and the boys marched out of the hut.

Smiling briefly at Jake, Orlando shrugged as though embarrassed by the performance and, by gestures, indicated that he could stay there or come with them as he chose. Jake did not feel like being alone again so soon, and anyway he was interested in seeing what they were going to do and so he followed the little army, picking up his bow and arrows, which had been dropped by the door in the scuffle. Orlando wanted to look at these. He felt the tips carefully and asked '*Venenosas?*' and Jake, without knowing the word but guessing what it meant, grinned and said 'Si', they were poisonous. Orlando nodded and Jake could tell he was impressed, which made him feel good, though he doubted if there really was any poison on the tips.

The children ran through the streets, dodging between buildings, down alleys and over patches of waste ground as though they were invisible. Sometimes they mingled with crowds for a moment before slipping through a gap in a fence and vanishing again. They seemed to know every inch of the city and also how to move in it so as to be inconspicuous. Jake simply did what they did and found that he became invisible too. There was one nasty moment when he saw a stall-holder's eyes widen in alarm as he noticed the bow and arrows and he stood rooted to the spot waiting for the man to shout and raise the alarm. But his arm was grabbed and he was out of sight again before any sound came out of the open mouth. Looking back from further up the street he could see the man still staring at the spot where he had been, scratching his head and with his mouth still hanging open.

Many of the shops were now shutting up for the day. Men were pulling down metal grills over windows and fixing padlocks on doors. The crowds in the streets were thinning by the time they had reached the farther side of the town. They stopped near a big modern supermarket which stood by itself inside a compound. Around the back there was a hole in the fence through which they all squeezed. Creeping past some outhouses they came in sight of the service entrance to the store. There was a loading bay for trucks with double doors behind. Orlando pointed out that there was a narrow gap between the top of the doors and the ceiling. That was how they were going to get in, he mimed.

Just as they were about to run across the last bit of open ground, a man came out of the back of the loading bay, pulled a chair out of the shadows and sat down in it. He was smoking a small cigar and he had a rifle. The boys froze and then retreated slowly round the corner. Once out of sight, they all looked at Orlando expectantly. He would find some way of dealing with this unexpected setback, they were sure. It was not going to be easy, as to rob the supermarket would take time and that would mean more than just distracting the guard's attention. Orlando was lost in thought. Then Jake had an idea. He held up the bow and pretended to shoot an arrow. Orlando shook his head, drawing his finger across his throat. It was then Jake's turn to mime that he did not intend hurting the guard. Now Orlando nodded.

Very cautiously, Jake crept back round the corner and crawled on his stomach to the nearest point to the loading bay. The guard was leaning back in his chair against a wooden upright. The smoke from his cigar rose straight into the air. 'No wind to allow for,' thought Jake, fitting an arrow to the bow. He aimed very carefully and let fly.

The arrow hit the wooden post with a twang they could all hear and the guard leapt to his feet, knocking his chair over. For an instant he stared at the arrow in total amazement. Then he let out a shriek, dropped his gun and ran to the gate in the fence. Fumbling with his keys, it took him several moments to unlock them, during which he kept glancing over his shoulder. Then he was through and running for his life down the road.

The boys came whooping out of hiding making Indian war cries, slapped Jake enthusiastically on the back and raced for the loading bay. There he retrieved his arrow while Orlando helped the smallest boy climb over the double doors. He was just able to squeeze through the gap and they heard him drop down on the far side. As they waited one of the boys picked up the guard's gun, but Orlando told him sharply to put it down and he obeyed at once. A moment later he had pulled the bolt back and they were all inside.

For starving boys it was a wonderland. Each grabbed a trolley and they dashed up and down the aisles throwing in anything they could reach. Mostly they went for biscuits, fruit and milk, Jake noticed, some of them even eating things as they ran. They really are hungry, he thought. He concentrated on tins, reckoning they would last longer and be more useful in the long run. One of the boys had been left outside as lookout and he started banging on the doors just as they heard police sirens approaching. As one they turned for the exit and shot out the back, each one wheeling his trolley at full speed.

They all made it across the compound and out of the gates before the first police car arrived and were just out of sight in some waste ground as it drove up. Orlando seemed to know the place already and led them down a bumpy slope, where a lot of things bounced out, to a dried-up river bed where there was hard sand on which the trolleys moved more easily. They sped along until they reached a concrete drain entering from the side, like the one they had run up that morning. Turning into it they hid the trolleys and then, under Orlando's direction, tore up bushes and ran back along the river bed wiping out their tracks.

On their return to the drain along the hillside, so as to leave no more tracks, they lay gasping for breath for a while before falling on the food again like hungry wolves. Jake, who was not particularly hungry, sat down and started opening tins with the attachment on his knife. Again he saw, as Orlando watched him, how much he wanted the knife, but he knew that they were now friends and that he could trust him absolutely not to steal it, even though he survived by stealing from others.

For an hour or so they gorged themselves. Then, when they could eat and drink no more, they hid most of what was left in the back of the drain.

Orlando wanted to leave it all, which Jake could not understand, and he insisted that they carry at least some in a couple of carrier bags which he had pinched. Reluctantly Orlando agreed.

It was not until they were halfway home that Jake discovered why the other boy had been right. Without knowing how it came about in the dark, and disorientated in the unfamiliar city, he suddenly found that they were surrounded by a gang of older boys. There must have been an unwritten agreement between the gangs that they could pass through their territories as long as they were empty handed and Jake had made them break this. The little ones huddled together and he could see that for the first time since he had met them they were frightened. The older boys were advancing from all sides.

Orlando gathered up all the food they were carrying and placed it on the ground in front of them; then he asked a question. The answer was clearly 'no', which in Brazilian sounded to Jake like an angry cat miaowing 'Nao'. The children started to shiver. It looked as though they were going to be beaten up.

Jake stepped forward holding an arrow half drawn in his bow. The boys stopped. Orlando stepped forward as well beside him and said something, of which Jake only understood two words '*Venenosas*' and '*Indio*'. The older boys backed away and there was a gap for the little ones to run through, which they did on a command from Orlando. Then he and Jake followed them, walking side by side, Jake pointing the bow, Orlando holding one of the arrows at the ready. Once clear, they ran faster than they had all day, but the other boys did not follow them and Jake felt that they might give Orlando and his gang a little more space in future.

That night Jake drew a Union Jack for Orlando and began to explain to him what he wanted to do.

they had all day, for the other boys did not follow
them, and it may be that they might over-balance
and his gang a little more peace in future.
That night Jake drew a plan for Orlando
and began to explain to him what he wanted to do.

20
The House

They spent the next day working together at the
desk, since they had agreed that it was too dangerous to attempt Jake's plan in daylight. He had really
grown to like Orlando and tried his best to teach
him everything he could think of that might be
useful. He drew him maps of the world and of
Brazil, listed all the languages he could remember
and in a mixture of Spanish and mime told him the
story of his own adventures. He was astonished by
how bright Orlando was and how quickly he
grasped things. He kept asking questions, too. Like
what were punctuation marks in writing, how did
one write a letter and address an envelope and how
did engines work? They were not easy questions to
answer without a common language but Jake tried
to answer them as best he could.

Two of the little boys went out during the day and
returned with a stale loaf of bread and some rotting
fruit which they all shared and at last the evening
approached. This was it. If he succeeded in his plan
he would soon be home; if he failed he might never
see his parents again. Jake's heart was thumping as
he gathered his few remaining things together and
prepared to leave the hut never, he hoped, to

return. Surprisingly none of the children had tried to steal his hat and he was glad of that as, if he ever did get back into a world where there was money and post offices, he wanted to send it back to Jaime. He put it firmly on his head, picked up the bow and arrows, made sure his knife was in his pocket and followed Orlando's troupe outside.

This time they headed uphill, away from the centre of town and into leafy and relatively prosperous suburbs. This was unfamiliar territory for the boys and dangerous too, as many of the houses had guards and guard dogs which barked as they passed. But they were still brilliant at slipping along invisibly and hiding when danger threatened. Jake had a pretty good idea where the house with the Union Jack was but it still took them a long time to find it. The big houses all looked the same from close to and it was difficult to see what flags they were flying in the still evening air. Then a breeze got up and suddenly there it was, billowing out in a garden below them.

The front gates were locked and there was a strong fence all round the garden. The boys examined it and found a weak spot where they started digging until there was almost room for him to get under. At that moment they heard furious barking and a large black Labrador charged up to them and started sniffing at where they had been digging. The boys were frightened and ran off, but Jake had a Labrador at home and thought he could probably deal with this one.

He had noticed an overflowing dustbin outside one of the houses they had passed. He and Orlando walked back to it and began to rummage. It was not a nice job, though he realized it was not the first time Orlando had done it, and it was some time before he found what he was looking for. It was some very smelly meat, which had gone off and been thrown away but was just the sort of thing a dog would fancy. Holding his nose with one hand, he picked it all up with the other and ran back to the fence. The dog was still there and growled menacingly.

Now Jake began to talk to the dog soothingly, holding a piece of meat at the same time. It sniffed suspiciously but wouldn't take it from his hand. 'Fetch!' he whispered, and threw the piece out onto the lawn. The dog pricked up its ears, hesitated for a moment and then dashed off joyfully to retrieve. Once the meat was in its mouth it was, of course, impossible not to eat it and once that was done it came panting back for more. Now it regarded Jake as a friend and even helped with the final bit of digging, being rewarded with more of the meat.

Just as Jake was about to crawl through, outside lights came on, a car's engine started up and the dog raced off across the lawn barking cheerfully. The boys all lay flat as the headlights swept over them. The car paused while the gates were opened and closed and then vanished down the street. The dog then came back panting harder and ready for more play.

Now it was time for Jake to say goodbye. His new friends could not come with him and he knew he was unlikely ever to see them again. The little ones gathered round him to hug and punch him affectionately. They had accepted him completely as their leader's friend. Orlando just shook his hand in his stiff dignified way and, after Jake had slipped under the wire and turned back for a last look, bowed as he had when they first met. Then all Jake's concentration was on getting to the other side of the lawn without being seen by any guards who might be about. He felt a bit foolish crawling on his stomach while the big black Labrador padded amiably along beside him, but he did it anyway and at last reached the flower beds along the wall of the house. Creeping along the edge of these, he came to a fire escape and, telling the dog to sit, in case he tried to come too, he began to climb up it.

The windows on the first floor were dark and locked. Above him, on the second floor, was a lighted window, and it was open. Very cautiously he climbed up to it and looked in. A young, fair-haired girl was sitting up in bed reading. Looking at her he was sure she was English. Without thinking what an alarming sight he must be, filthy dirty and dressed in rags, he stepped into the room and said 'Hello. My name is Jake Travis and I've been in the jungle for rather a long time.'

The girl's eyes widened and he thought for a moment that she was about to scream. Then she said very calmly 'How did you get past Bumble? He's meant to be such a good guard dog.'

'I gave him some meat. Then I told him to sit so that he wouldn't try to climb the fire escape.'

'That was clever. Now tell me about the jungle. Daddy won't let me go into it as he says it's danger-ous. Gosh! You're not the boy who was kidnapped are you? Everyone's been looking for you.'

'I suppose I am. Do you know where my father is?'

'I don't, but Daddy will. He's the British Consul. He and Mummy have just gone out to dinner. Why don't you go and have a bath? You stink, I can smell you from here. You can put on some of my brother's clothes. His room's next door but he's away at school. My name's Lizzie, by the way, and I'm eight.'

And so, when the British Consul and his wife went up to check on their daughter after getting back from dinner, they found a very clean and presentable twelve-year-old dressed in their son's clothes and sitting at the foot of their daughter's bed telling her tall stories about the Amazon rainforest.

On the way to the airport to meet his father's plane, Jake sat in the back of the black chauffeur-driven limousine with Lizzie. She had insisted on going too. 'After all, I found him,' she said and Jake had said he wanted her along. They had also managed to hide nearly all her school books under the back seat while the car was parked in the drive.

They told the driver to take an unusual way into town and at a certain point made him stop. It was a district usually avoided by respectable people and he was not happy about this but he had learnt that it was no use arguing with Lizzie. The two children got out carrying a large pile of books, walked across the road and disappeared through a broken fence. The chauffeur thought he had better get out and follow. Peering through the fence he was amazed to see his charges surrounded by some of the most verminous creatures he had ever set eyes on. They were leaping about like dervishes, taking the books off Jake and Lizzie and carrying them inside a run-down hut. Jake and a strange, taller boy with start-ling white hair above scarred black skin, were stand-ing face to face. The chauffeur saw Jake pass him something small and bright red; then the two English children were back at the fence and crossing to the car.

'It's all right, Manuel,' said Lizzie. 'We can go to the airport now.'

The first words Jake said to his father as he hugged him were 'Dad, can I have a new Swiss Army knife, please?'

Epilogue

Jake found that he was quite a celebrity, as the news of his kidnap had been carried by papers all over the world and the Peruvian authorities had made great efforts to find him for the five weeks he had been missing. Several *Sendero Luminoso* guerrilla groups had been captured, including the one led by the girl Maria, but she had managed to escape before she was put in prison. Under interrogation, the others had admitted that they had taken Jake but that he had run off into the jungle. The area around their camp had been thoroughly searched but when no trace of Jake had been found, most people had eventually concluded that he must have been eaten by some wild animal. His father had never given up. It *had* been him in the search plane which Jake had seen and he had also followed the track through the forest for some distance, convinced that his son was not far away; but he had never found any of the camp sites and so he had never been sure.

The search area had been widened and his father had even visited the village where the massacre had taken place. That had caused a great scandal and seemed to have been the work of a renegade unit of the Peruvian army, not of the *Sendero Luminoso* as everyone had at first thought. It was all to do with the murky world of drug smuggling. When Jake dcscribed how he had been there and had escaped in a smuggler's boat, his father went pale at the thought of how much danger he had been in.

'I think you have been very brave and resourceful,' he said and for Jake it suddenly all seemed to have been worth it.

The Lopez family had been wonderfully kind, helping in every possible way and saying that it was all their fault since they had persuaded Jake and his father to visit them and anyway it was Jaime the guerrillas had been after. Jake rang Jaime from the airport while waiting for the flight home and made him promise to come over with his family to stay during the next holidays. He had, of course, already called his mother from the consulate soon after Lizzie's parents had found him.

A special message arrived from the captain of the QE2 saying that the whole crew were over the moon to know that he was safe and inviting him and his father to join them again on the next world cruise.

'Perhaps we'll have another adventure,' said Jake.

'I do hope not!' said his father. They did, but that's another story.

Animal Notes

These are some of the creatures Jake met in the Amazon rainforest.

Jaguar (*Panthera onca*). The third largest of all the big cats (after the tiger and the lion), they can be 1.8m long without their tails and can weigh up to 135 kg. They can crush a man's skull with a single blow but seldom attack unprovoked. Their favourite food is peccaries and they also catch fish, attracting them by dangling their tails in the water and then scooping them out. (See p. 42)

Coati mundi (*Nasua Nasua*). Racoonlike mammal which roams the forest floor, sometimes in bands of up to 40. They have long banded tails and flexible, elongated snouts, with which they probe cracks in search of food. (See p. 43)

Spider monkey (*Ateles spp.*). Only in the New World have some monkeys evolved prehensile tails to give them extra stability as they swing through the trees. The inside of the tip is bare of fur so that they can hang from it leaving their hands and feet free for feeding on the fruit which is their staple diet. (See p. 46)

Blue and gold macaw (*Ara ararauna*). One of the most spectacular birds of South America, they are usually seen in pairs but sometimes in flocks of up to 50. They are large and very noisy, making a raucous screech which echoes through the forest. (See p. 51)

Howler monkey (*Alouatta*). The most widespread and among the largest of all South American monkeys. They sing in chorus in the mornings and evenings. The males have a sound box in their throats which inflates to produce an incredibly loud noise, which can be heard several kilometres away. It may be the loudest noise made by any animal on earth and is very frightening. (See p. 52)

Hornet (*Vespidae spp.*). Largest of the social wasps, hornets build paper nests above the ground. Their sting, which injects formic acid into their victim, is one of the more painful rainforest experiences and can leave a lasting scar. But the hornets give clear warning that they should be avoided by displaying the danger colours yellow and black. There are, of course, many harmless insects which imitate these colours in order to be left alone. (See p. 61)

Red piranha (*Serrusalmus nattereri*). Most piranha are either vegetarian or relatively harmless, but red piranha are predatory with formidably sharp triangular teeth. A shoal of hundreds, each tearing off a chunk of flesh, can reduce an animal as large as a cow to bare bones in a few minutes. (See p. 66)

Capybaras (*Hydrochoerus*). The largest of all rodents. They have webbed hoofs and no tail. Well over a metre long and weighing up to 75 kg, they spend most of their time in the water feeding on plants. Shy and completely harmless, they can stay under water for several minutes. (See p. 69)

White-lipped peccary (*Tayassu pecaru*). Boar-like

animal that roams deep in the Amazon rainforest in herds of 50 to 100. Normally they root about in the soil grubbing up plants, insects and even snakes. They can be aggressive, attacking and killing creatures larger than themselves. (See p. 70)

Jigger (*Tunga penetrans*). A small flea which burrows under the skin, often between the toes. Only pregnant females do this and the resulting maggot-like larvae can cause nasty infections if not treated promptly. (See p. 88)

Giant anteater (*Myrmecophaga*). The biggest of all the anteaters, they are about 2 metres long, with huge, hairy tails. They have no teeth but the powerful claws on their forelegs can tear open the hardest termite hills and their long tongues can probe deep inside the passages. (See p. 90)